Perfect Mendacity

by Jason Wells

A SAMUEL FRENCH ACTING EDITION

SAMUEL
FRENCH

FOUNDED 1830

NEW YORK HOLLYWOOD LONDON TORONTO

SAMUELFRENCH.COM

ISBN 978-0-573-69846-0   Printed in U.S.A.   #29664

MUSIC USE NOTE

IMPORTANT BILLING AND CREDIT
REQUIREMENTS

PERFECT MENDACITY was produced at the Steppenwolf Theatre in Chicago, Illinois on July 26, 2008, as part of the First Look Repertory of New Work. The project director was Edward Sobel. The performance was directed by David Cromer, with sets by Kevin Depinet, costumes by Debbie Baer, lighting by Charles Cooper, sound by Joseph Fosco, dramaturgy by Rachel Walshe, and fight choreography by Joe Dempsey. The production stage manager was Kathleen Petroziello. The cast was as follows:

WALTER KREUTZER.................................Matt DeCaro
D'AVORE PEOPLES.......................... Aaron Todd Douglas
SAMIRA KREUTZER ....Liza Fernandez
ROGER STANHOPE ....Tim Curtis
DR. DOLL ....Scott Aiello

PERFECT MENDACITY opened at the Asolo Repertory Theatre in Sarasota, Florida on May 15, 2009. The performance was directed by Michael Donald Edwards, with sets by Jeffrey W. Dean, costumes by June Elisabeth Taylor, lighting by Aaron Muhl, and sound by Kevin Kennedy. The production stage manager was Marian Wallace. The cast was as follows:

WALTER KREUTZER.............................David Breitbarth
D'AVORE PEOPLES.............................DeMario McGrew
SAMIRA KREUTZER ....Diana Simonzadeh
ROGER STANHOPE ....Douglas Jones
DR. DOLL ....Jason Peck

CHARACTERS

WALTER KREUTZER – 50s, white American
D'AVORE PEOPLES – 40s, black American
SAMIRA KREUTZER – 30s or 40s, Moroccan
ROGER STANHOPE – 50s, white South African
DR. DOLL

SETTING

D'Avore Peoples' office
A suburban condo
A laboratory office

TIME

The Present

AUTHOR'S NOTE

The slash (/) indicates the point at which an overlap begins. That is, the actor with the next line will begin speaking at this point.

To Karen

Scene One

(**WALTER KREUTZER** *and* **D'AVORE PEOPLES**. *Peoples' office.*)

PEOPLES. Countermeasures.

WALTER. Right.

PEOPLES. That's what we call them. You been on the internet, right?

WALTER. Yes.

PEOPLES. Of course. But you come to me because you wanta cut through all the…

WALTER. Mmhm.

PEOPLES. All the *debris*. Of information.

WALTER. There's a lot of…contradictory…

PEOPLES. Information. Rigged for maximum, you know, sensationalism.

WALTER. It seems so.

PEOPLES. Everyone wants to think they know something.

WALTER. Well, your website said you had some experience in this area.

PEOPLES. Oh, and I do. I don't lie.

WALTER. Hm.

PEOPLES. And I am experienced enough to tell you that it's *very* difficult to beat a good polygraph examiner. Notice I said "examiner."

WALTER. Right.

PEOPLES. People think a polygraph is a machine that tells you if you're lying. Like it just says "true" or "false" and that's it. But that is not what it is.

WALTER. Right.

PEOPLES. You know this.

7

WALTER. Sure.

PEOPLES. The polygraph is a tool. Used by an examiner. Who studies the information before him and reaches a conclusion, which constitutes his personal opinion. If the examiner is good, there is no guaranteed method of deceiving him. And you should always assume that he will be good. Who is he?

WALTER. I don't know.

PEOPLES. I can provide you with a list of bad ones. Perhaps you could insist on one of them. Do you have a choice?

WALTER. No.

PEOPLES. Then you should start by complaining that you don't have a choice.

WALTER. I suppose I can bring it up. But you said no "guaranteed" way. But there are *ways*, right?

PEOPLES. What sort of trouble are you in?

WALTER. I told you on the phone… I'm embroiled in a divorce…situation.

PEOPLES. Divorce. Right.

WALTER. Right.

PEOPLES. And what about this divorce do you wish to lie about?

WALTER. Well. "Lie." I mean… It's a complicated financial issue.

PEOPLES. It is.

WALTER. I'd really rather not go into a lot of detail.

PEOPLES. I see.

WALTER. I'm obviously not totally comfortable with…with going into a lot of detail.

PEOPLES. Okay. Well…in any divorce case, your attorney would have the right to approve the examiner.

WALTER. I'd rather not pursue that, if I can avoid it. I'd rather appear…accommodating…if I can.

PEOPLES. Mmhm.

WALTER. I don't want to appear to *hedge*.

PEOPLES. So, refusing the examination…that's out of the question.

WALTER. I'm afraid so.

PEOPLES. Even though it is your legal right to do so. In any and all cases.

WALTER. Yes.

PEOPLES. This must be a very ugly divorce.

WALTER. Yeah.

PEOPLES. For a man still wearing his ring.

WALTER. Yeah. So can you help me?

PEOPLES. I can tell you how to mess up the results. Mess 'em up bad, without tipping your hand. In most cases, "Inconclusive" is as good as NDI – No Deception Indicated. "Inconclusive" will sometimes do the job.

WALTER. I have to *pass.*

PEOPLES. Listen to me. You can set out to mess up the test, which is relatively easy. Or you can set out to *pass,* which is much, much harder. But these are two mutually exclusive processes. If you set out to pass and you fall short, you don't get "Inconclusive" for a consolation prize. You get DI – Deception Indicated. And that's the last thing you want. Am I right?

WALTER. It is my carefully considered belief that an inconclusive test will not end my problems. I have to *take* this test and I have to *pass* it.

PEOPLES. Let's go down the list, so that you can understand that we've thought of everything. Forget about drugs. Drugs leave a fingerprint, right on the graph, to anyone who can read it. Same goes for hypnosis. You've got to be alert and in control. Physical countermeasures: problematic. They look for muscle-flexing. Jaw movement. They got a pad that you sit on, it detects the constriction of your sphincter muscle. Now, when somebody goes and invents a device that detects the constriction of your sphincter muscle, this tells us two things: that physical countermeasures *work,* and that your examiner is salivating to catch you squeezing up your butthole. So it's a trade-off, see. And since the internet wasn't good enough for you, you must need the best. That's why you come to me, right? Hell, yes. This countermeasure has to be undetectable. We have to use psychology. I'm going to teach you my personal, exclusive method for how to work that machine with only the power of your imagination.

WALTER. Should I take notes?

PEOPLES. For the time being, we'll just have a conversation. Okay?

WALTER. Okay.

PEOPLES. But if you really want my help, it would behoove you to tell me what you did.

WALTER. I didn't do anything. I mean…I didn't…I'm not…

PEOPLES. / Drink some water.

WALTER. I…I didn't do anything *bad*. I'm not a bad person.

PEOPLES. I'm sure that's true. But let's start with what you did.

WALTER. I need to know that I can trust you.

PEOPLES. I don't know how I can help you with that. But I know you're not gonna get your money's worth unless you do.

WALTER. I'm just – I'm just – I'm just not prepared…to…

PEOPLES. You've seen my website: eight years in law enforcement, nine years as a polygraph consultant… I wouldn't last long if I was indiscreet, now would I? What would happen if I started turning in my clients?

WALTER. Sure. Sure. But, um, this information would be very valuable to certain people.

PEOPLES. Is that right?

WALTER. Yes.

PEOPLES. Well, now you're putting ideas in my head.

WALTER. I – I'm sorry? I –

PEOPLES. I'm just joking with you. Look, if you gonna pass this polygraph, you gonna have to trust someone.

WALTER. Aren't the rules of, of beating the polygraph, aren't they going to be the same, whatever the situation?

PEOPLES. How we gonna practice? If I don't know what to ask you?

WALTER. We're gonna practice?

PEOPLES. Sure, we're gonna practice. I've got a unit right here. State of the art. Almost.

WALTER. Okay. I don't want to offend you. But until we get to that point, can we just keep the discussion…in *generalities?*

PEOPLES. That's fine. No offense taken. Trust everyone, but cut the cards, right? Who said that?

WALTER. I don't know.

PEOPLES. I'll look it up later. Now, let me ask you: What is the one and only…reality…which has permeated human behavior since the beginning of humankind. So indelible in our psychology, that even a tiny child will teach himself to do it with no adult intervention whatsoever?

WALTER. Lying?

PEOPLES. *(his thunder stolen)* Well. Yes. You must be a very intelligent man.

WALTER. Well. It *was* the subject at hand.

PEOPLES. Yes. *Lying.* The ability to keep our own secrets. And there are some who would seek to take this human gift from us.

WALTER. Mr. Peoples:

PEOPLES. Now:

WALTER. Mr. Peoples: With all / due respect…

PEOPLES. You're cramping my style. This is part of the training.

WALTER. Really.

PEOPLES. Yes. Because if you want to beat the polygraph, you gotta go in there with a fundamental belief in your right to lie.

WALTER. I see.

PEOPLES. The polygraph is a machine that measures stress. And the more that you are persuaded by its infallibility, the greater will be your stress at lying to it.

WALTER. I read that.

PEOPLES. It's an instrument of propaganda. If you believe the propaganda, you will fail.

WALTER. Hm.

PEOPLES. The examiner will dazzle you with science. He'll claim a ninety-eight percent success rate. Make it seem hopeless. Undermine your confidence.

WALTER. Yes.

PEOPLES. Let's say your company has experienced a theft, and one hundred employees are given a polygraph. Okay?

WALTER. Yeah.

PEOPLES. Now let's say the examiner picks the wrong fellow. That fellow is fired, his life is ruined, and the thief goes free. Now, you would call that a complete catastrophe, would you not?

WALTER. Yes.

PEOPLES. Well, the examiner will *not* call it a complete catastrophe; he will call it a ninety-eight percent success. 'Cause he tested a hundred people, and was only wrong *twice.* You see?

WALTER. Wow.

PEOPLES. Wow indeed, Dr. Krootzer.

WALTER. What?

PEOPLES. Mr. Jamison. I forgot to call you Mr. Jamison.

WALTER. How did you know my name?

PEOPLES. I beg your pardon. Never mind.

WALTER. How do you know my name?

PEOPLES. Well. I'm the black private dick that's a sex machine for all the chicks.

WALTER. What?

PEOPLES. I'm Shaft, baby.

Okay. Never mind. But, you would think, my line of business, a lot of people would want to pay cash, right? But you'd be wrong. You're the first ever. So, just for fun, you understand, just to entertain myself, I thought I'd run your cell phone number, and you know what I found, right? It's a pre-pay. Man with enough money he's worried his wife's gonna get it, you didn't sound to me like a pre-pay kind of guy. So, I'm like dang, his wife must have *some lawyers*, he goes out and gets a pre-pay phone. So, just because it's a challenge for me now, you understand, just for fun I had my niece run out and mark down your plate numbers so I could run your plates while you was waiting.

WALTER. Is that why I had to wait so long?

PEOPLES. I'm sorry about that. Sometimes I can't help myself. But you must have more confidence in me now, don't you think, see how *competent* I am.

WALTER. You said "Doctor." It doesn't say "Doctor" on my driver's license.

PEOPLES. Dang. You are very perceptive. Well, I run your name through Google, turns out you're a respected botanist or…botanical…*scientist* or something. And I run you through YouTube, turns out you been on Fox News a bunch of times, talking about terrorists and whatnot.

WALTER. Oh, my God.

PEOPLES. It's all right. We were gonna have to get there anyway. I'm just helping the relationship along.

WALTER. What happened to my fundamental right to keep my secrets?

PEOPLES. I don't pay attention to irony. I'm a Christian man. Now, shall I call you Jamison, or Krootzer?

WALTER. Kreutzer.

PEOPLES. Kroyster?

WALTER. Kroyt-zer.

PEOPLES. I'm gonna call you Walter. Now, Walter: What did you do?

WALTER. I work for a large, private contracting firm. Chenoweth. As you probably already know.

PEOPLES. I didn't get that far. I couldn't keep you waiting.

WALTER. Yes. Well, someone leaked confidential information to the media. Chenoweth wants to know who did it.

PEOPLES. And when you say "someone," you mean *you.*

WALTER. No.

PEOPLES. No? Then what are we talking about?

WALTER. They're going to ask me if I know who did it.

PEOPLES. So just tell 'em who did it. You can't lose your job for someone else.

WALTER. Yes, I can.

PEOPLES. How?

WALTER. Because I think it was my wife.

PEOPLES. Your wife works at Chewbaccawhatsit?

WALTER. No.

PEOPLES. Then how did your wife get confidential information?

WALTER. From me.

PEOPLES. And she ran off to the media with it?

WALTER. I think so.

PEOPLES. Did you ask her?

WALTER. No.

PEOPLES. Why not?

WALTER. I'm… I'm afraid.

PEOPLES. You're afraid of your wife?

WALTER. I'm afraid she'll say she did it. Then I'll know. And I'll fail the test.

PEOPLES. That ain't how it works. You're gonna fail the test anyhow, because you *think* you know.

WALTER. I know.

PEOPLES. So why don't you ask your wife? Maybe she'll say she didn't do it.

WALTER. I think she did it.

PEOPLES. Why don't you ask her?

WALTER. I'm...Maybe I'm just afraid.

PEOPLES. Afraid of your wife.

WALTER. Maybe.

PEOPLES. What kind of secrets are we talking about?

WALTER. I'd rather not say.

PEOPLES. You said it's already in the media.

WALTER. I'm not comfortable discussing it.

PEOPLES. You know I'm just gonna look it up.

WALTER. Fine.

PEOPLES. Something illegal?

WALTER. Not in *this* country. But unsavory.

PEOPLES. 'Cause we got whistleblower laws.

WALTER. How does *that* work?

PEOPLES. I have no idea. But if your company was doing something illegal, there must be protections.

WALTER. My work is Government Classified.

PEOPLES. *Huh.* Like Top Secret?

WALTER. Well, "Classified." But *like* that. Yes.

PEOPLES. Okay. That's a problem. They gonna arrest you for treason?

WALTER. No. I don't think so.

PEOPLES. You're not a traitor to your country, are you?

WALTER. Absolutely not.

PEOPLES. 'Cause I gotta draw the line somewhere.

WALTER. I'm not a traitor. But I signed an ironclad non-disclosure agreement. Whistleblower or no, I'll be in court for the rest of my life, and my career as a micro-biologist...not *botanist*, by the way... It'll be over.

PEOPLES. And you're not even a whistleblower.

WALTER. I'm not?

PEOPLES. No. Your wife is.

WALTER. Right. So…

PEOPLES. So you don't even have that.

WALTER. Right.

PEOPLES. So this is bad for you.

WALTER. My point exactly. The best way, the *only* way, is simply: pass the test. And I'm clear.

PEOPLES. Or turn the woman in.

WALTER. What?

PEOPLES. Turn the woman in, and I bet they'll make a deal with you.

WALTER. *Maybe.* But they won't make a deal with *her.* They'll go after her.

PEOPLES. They *might* make a deal with her. To avoid publicity, / or…

WALTER. I don't think so. She's Moroccan.

PEOPLES. Uh huh. So?

WALTER. That's…she's…Arab.

PEOPLES. Oh. She's not, uh…

WALTER. "Political"?

PEOPLES. …In a religious, sort of… / way?

WALTER. *No.* And *no.* She's a simple woman.

PEOPLES. And you sure you don't wanta just throw her to the wolves?

WALTER. No. What / kind of a…

PEOPLES. Easy now, Walter. / I just…

WALTER. I'm not here to… / throw my wife…

PEOPLES. Easy. I just have to assess all the particulars.

WALTER. I just want to pass the test. I just want to keep the life I have now. That's all.

PEOPLES. Okay, Walter. Drink some water. We're gonna get to work.

You know about method actors?

WALTER. Method actors?

PEOPLES. Yeah. Method actors. How they use psychology to play a part.

WALTER. I guess so. Yeah.

PEOPLES. What they do is, when they're supposed to feel something, a particular thing, they think of something in their own life makes 'em feel that way. Okay?

WALTER. Okay.

PEOPLES. So that it's real, okay? Not just faking it, right?

WALTER. Yeah.

PEOPLES. But when they *need* it, they gotta come up with it right away. They don't have time to sit there and *conjure* it all the time, you know?

WALTER. Yeah.

PEOPLES. That's what *you* gotta do. You gotta turn it on, turn it off, just like that. So what they do, the method actors, they attach an image to that feeling. A single, powerful image that represents that feeling. You following me?

WALTER. I guess so.

PEOPLES. It's not enough to see your father whuppin' you, even if he whupped you every day. It's too general. That feeling has to be, has to be, *distilled.* Into a single image, something that makes you feel that terror, that anxiety, every time, without fail. The ring on his finger. A spot of plaster on the tip of his shoe. A, uh…a vein in his eyeball. You gotta contemplate that beating all the time, every day, and as soon as you feel that anxiety, your mind has to go straight to that ring, that shoe, whatever, right away, every time. Until you have *attached* that image to that anxiety. So that when you produce that image, you will instantly produce that feeling. Do you see?

WALTER. Like Pavlov's dog.

PEOPLES. Okay. Now *what* is that?

WALTER. The dog got fed whenever it heard a bell. So, eventually…

PEOPLES. Right, right. / The dog…

WALTER. The dog would salivate, / whenever…

PEOPLES. Yeah, would salivate whenever it heard the bell. I heard about that. *What's* that dog's name?

WALTER. Uh. *Pavlov's* dog.

PEOPLES. The *dog's* got a name, don't he?

WALTER. I don't know the dog's name.

PEOPLES. I'll look it up. But that's right. It's just like the dog. You gotta salivate when you hear the bell. That's what the method actors do. You understand? This technique, *my* technique, the one I'm gonna teach you, it's all in the mind. It's pure. It's undetectable.

WALTER. And it works?

PEOPLES. Every person I have trained in this technique, who has absorbed it with the proper seriousness, has passed his or her polygraph examination. I guarantee that.

WALTER. Do you have testimonials?

PEOPLES. Testimonials? Hell yes, I got a million testimonials.

WALTER. People I can contact?

PEOPLES. People you – Now, how I'm gonna do that? You think these people want to be contacted?

WALTER. Well, then – Well, I'm kind of taking your word for it, then.

PEOPLES. I already told you, I don't lie. And if I *did* lie, I would have you give me a polygraph which I would pass, thereby proving to you that I don't lie. Now, you can't argue with that.

WALTER. Isn't there anyone I can talk to who has used this technique successfully, in the real world?

PEOPLES. You're getting off track, Walter, and you're missing the point. Which is that I know of which I speak. And you are going to pass this test with flying colors and you are going to say, "I did this with the help of my new friend, Mr. D'avore Peoples, and his magnificent method of the power of the mind over technology."

WALTER. It just sounds, kind of…

> **(PEOPLES** *sighs.)*

> …sketchy.

PEOPLES. Walter, let me ask you something, alright?

> Do you have a *choice?*

> Now, get out that pen. The time has come for you to take some notes.

> *(blackout)*

End of Scene

Scene Two

(An upper-middle class condo; the home of **WALTER** *and* **SAMIRA KREUTZER**.)

*(***SAMIRA** *sits, holding a packet of papers. She is reading from one of the pages, though this may not be clear to us for a moment.)*

SAMIRA. "Have you ever lied to get yourself out of trouble?" "Have you ever stolen anything from work?" "Have you ever betrayed a friend?" "Have you ever lied to your supervisor?" "Have you ever cheated on your taxes?" "Do you dislike black people?" "Do you sometimes dis– despair…"?

WALTER. *(offstage)* "Disparage."

SAMIRA. "…disparage people of other ethnic groups?" "Have you ever claimed credit for something when it was not deserved?"

WALTER. *(offstage)* Are you going to read them all?

SAMIRA. These are very undignified.

*(***WALTER** *enters from the bathroom, drying his face with a towel.)*

WALTER. Yes.

SAMIRA. Why would they ask you questions like these?

WALTER. To see what I do when I lie.

SAMIRA. "Have you ever betrayed someone who trusted you?"

WALTER. Samira. Please.

SAMIRA. It's embarrassing.

WALTER. *Yes.*

SAMIRA. You should refuse to answer.

WALTER. But I can't do that. Can I.

SAMIRA. I don't know.

WALTER. No. I can't.

SAMIRA. Why not?

WALTER. You know why not. They'll fire me. They could even prosecute me.

SAMIRA. But you didn't do anything.

WALTER. No.

SAMIRA. So they can't persecute you.

WALTER. *Prosecute* me.

SAMIRA. Prosecute you.

WALTER. But they can fire me. *And* persecute me.

SAMIRA. So what if they do. They're evil.

WALTER. They're not evil. I don't know why you say that. But what if they are? How am I supposed to make a living?

SAMIRA. You can teach.

WALTER. Who's going to hire me? If I've been fired for – as a suspect in some, in some breach of National Security.

SAMIRA. You exaggerate.

WALTER. I don't exaggerate, Samira. I don't *exaggerate*.

SAMIRA. I would like to move anyway.

WALTER. To where? "France"?

SAMIRA. Yes.

WALTER. Sip wine and eat croissants all day?

SAMIRA. Yes.

WALTER. We've discussed that.

SAMIRA. You don't like French people.

WALTER. No.

SAMIRA. Because they didn't want to go to war.

WALTER. That was just the…

SAMIRA. The what.

WALTER. The final straw.

SAMIRA. Because they weren't convinced by the evidence?

WALTER. I just don't want to go to France.

SAMIRA. …Because the evidence was *wrong*.

WALTER. You don't understand the subtleties. And I've got news for you: They have evil corporations in France, too.

SAMIRA. It is not news to me. I am quite aware of it. I know more about the French than you. I just want to live there.

WALTER. I have a job here.

(re: the papers)

Can I have that? I need to study those.

SAMIRA. They're going to ask you these?

WALTER. No. They're just examples. I have to learn to spot the control qu– the, the "comparison" questions without, you know, without hesitating.

SAMIRA. Why do they make you admit these things?

WALTER. I'm not supposed to admit them. I'm supposed to *deny* them.

SAMIRA. Why do they want you to deny them? They want to catch you?

WALTER. No. I mean, yes, they do, but that isn't it. I have to deny these things so they can, they can, measure my response when I lie.

SAMIRA. So you'll *deny* that you dislike black people?

WALTER. For example.

SAMIRA. …Which will be a lie?

WALTER. Are you…?

SAMIRA. What.

WALTER. Are you *picking* at me?

(She shrugs.)

What does that mean?

SAMIRA. I want to understand.

WALTER. They're not going to ask that.

SAMIRA. It's on your list.

WALTER. They'll go over the questions ahead of time. I can ask them to change the question.

SAMIRA. *Will* you ask them to change the question?

WALTER. What are you doing?

SAMIRA. Do you dislike Jewish people?

WALTER. What?

SAMIRA. They could ask you that, too.

WALTER. Possibly. Why are you acting like this?

SAMIRA. I'm trying to understand.

WALTER. They're not going to ask those things.

SAMIRA. It's on your list. I'm helping.

WALTER. You're not helping. You're trying to make me…

SAMIRA. What.

WALTER. I don't know. Feel foolish about something. I mean, are you *calling* me something?

SAMIRA. What would I be calling you?

WALTER. Okay. That's enough. We have Roger coming over.

SAMIRA. "We" do?

WALTER. Yes, "we" do. The two of us, who live here. Is this inconvenient for you?

SAMIRA. I'm tired. I didn't expect visitors.

WALTER. Really? So this *is* inconvenient for you. This situation, this *crisis*, that someone has created for me.

SAMIRA. You think *I* did this.

(*a beat*)

WALTER. (*cautiously*) Well?

SAMIRA. "Well" did I do it?

WALTER. I brought the memo home.

SAMIRA. Why?

WALTER. "Why?" Bec– What difference does it make?

SAMIRA. Why did you bring it home.

WALTER. To – It – It seemed valuable.

SAMIRA. For, what do you call it, "blackmail."

WALTER. No, that's not what I call it. I call it *leverage*, and it wasn't *leverage*, it was – I wanted to contemplate the *meaning* of it.

SAMIRA. For your conscience?

WALTER. No. Not for my *conscience*. To consider my *position*, in terms of legal…culpability, having seen the memo and not, you know, *acted*, and so forth.

SAMIRA. Why not for your conscience?

WALTER. Because it didn't *trouble* my conscience. I'm not a fool.

SAMIRA. You think I'm trying to trap you?

WALTER. Trap me how?

SAMIRA. If you say that it troubled your conscience and you didn't act on it, you think I'll say you're a coward. You would rather I think that you have no conscience at all, than think that you're scared. You would rather I think you approved of this memo.

WALTER. I didn't approve of it. I didn't *disapprove* of it. It was just a *thing*. An artifact of commerce. And why would I think that my wife wants to *trap* me into *confessing* to a *conscience*?

SAMIRA. To having a conscience and not *act*. Not *acting*. You think it's better to not have a conscience at all.

WALTER. No, I don't think that. I think *you* think that.

SAMIRA. And so this is why you think I'm trying to trap you.

WALTER. I'm – what?

SAMIRA. *I* can follow it. You can't follow it?

WALTER. No. I need to study these questions. / This is…

SAMIRA. And I don't think this, anyway. Is my point. It's better to *have* a conscience.

WALTER. And I do. I actually have one.

SAMIRA. You mean, you have a conscience, but you didn't *act*?

(She's trapped him.)

WALTER. What pleasure are you getting from this?

SAMIRA. Are you angry with me?

WALTER. I brought the memo *home*…

SAMIRA. I remember.

WALTER. I *told* you about it. You wanted to *see* it.

SAMIRA. So?

WALTER. So, a week later it's on the web.

SAMIRA. So?

WALTER. Is that all you have to say?

SAMIRA. Did you do it?

WALTER. Did I do what?

SAMIRA. Give it to the internet.

WALTER. Of course not. You know I didn't.

SAMIRA. Then someone else did.

WALTER. Yes. Someone else *did.*

SAMIRA. Others had the memo. The one on the internet may not be yours.

WALTER. Stop acting like you don't get it. It doesn't matter if it's mine. I wasn't supposed to bring it *home.*

SAMIRA. People make mistakes, dear, don't they? The important thing is that you did not give it to the internet. And you don't know who did.

WALTER. I don't?

SAMIRA. That's the important thing, yes?

WALTER. I don't know who did it, Samira?

SAMIRA. Good. And it's best that way.

(pause)

WALTER. Right. I have to work on this.

SAMIRA. Can I help?

WALTER. I don't think so.

SAMIRA. Why? What do you have to do?

WALTER. Okay. Um… Okay. I have to study these questions. These control questions. So th– "comparison" questions, so that I can, you know, *spot* them. Instantly. And push my, what he calls, my *red* button.

SAMIRA. What's your red button?

WALTER. My mental image. My red image. It's supposed to spike my reactions, draw a picture of a lie. Of *me*, lying. Then, when they ask a *relevant* question, I push my blue button, go to my "cool" image, suppress my natural reaction, see?

SAMIRA. I guess.

WALTER. So it won't match with the lie. It won't look like the lie, see?

SAMIRA. Oh.

WALTER. That's supposed to be the idea, anyway.

SAMIRA. Red questions and blue questions.

WALTER. And white. White ones are irrelevant: "Is your name Walter Kreutzer?" "Did you ever live in Africa?" That kind of thing. I push my white button. Blank page. Nothing. I see nothing.

SAMIRA. "Did you ever live in Africa?"

WALTER. Or whatever.

SAMIRA. That's not irrelevant, though.

WALTER. Yes. It's irrelevant. "Did you ever – " "Do you live at one-six-nine-three-nine Tidepool Court?" "Are your eyes blue?"

SAMIRA. These things seem relevant to me.

WALTER. Well, they're not. How could they be?

SAMIRA. A blue-eyed man has different lies than a brown-eyed man. Or a man who lives on Tidepool Court, or on Martin Luther King Drive…

WALTER. No, no. For God's sake, Samira. You're *way* over-thinking this.

SAMIRA. And *Africa*, especially. This is not irrelevant. They're going to ask you about Africa?

WALTER. No. They're *not*. These, these, these *questions*… I'm describing…they have no meaningful context. They are *trivia*. To cleanse the palate.

SAMIRA. If you say so, yes. But they seem meaningful to me. They might be trying to trick you with these.

WALTER. No. *No.* It's not a *trick*. These questions are not meant to be pondered for philosophical significance.

SAMIRA. If you say so.

WALTER. Yes. Of course. It's like, "Is the carpet gray?" Like that. Now, please don't make something / out of the…

SAMIRA. No. I understand.

WALTER. …Out of the / carpet…

SAMIRA. No, no.

WALTER. …Being gray.

SAMIRA. Yes. I see. They're not *intended* to have meaning.

WALTER. The white questions are meaningless.

SAMIRA. Yes.

WALTER. Yes.

SAMIRA. Except for Africa.

WALTER. What the *fuck*, Samira.

SAMIRA. Don't swear at me. If they / ask you about Africa…

WALTER. Even fucking Africa. What are you trying to say…? / What…?

SAMIRA. If they ask you about Africa…

WALTER. They're not going to ask me about fucking – It was / an *example*.

SAMIRA. Don't swear at me.

WALTER. …From my own *head*. In no way / relevant to…

SAMIRA. Why would you give that example?

WALTER. Because we lived in Africa. Why wouldn't I?

SAMIRA. You could talk too much about it.

WALTER. I'm not, I'm not – I won't be *extemporizing*, during the examination. I won't be free-associating. Okay?

(wary)

What did you think I was going to say about Africa?

SAMIRA. Everything means something.

WALTER. You've made this harder for me now, do you know that?

SAMIRA. No, please. Don't say that. I'm sorry. I want to help you, sweetheart. I just don't see why you can't tell the truth.

WALTER. Yes, you do. You *do* see.

SAMIRA. If you didn't want to send it, why did you bring it home? Why did you show it to me?

WALTER. I told you.

SAMIRA. I think you wanted to send it.

WALTER. Well, you are absolutely wrong.

SAMIRA. I'm giving you the doubt, anyway, the benefits of the doubt.

WALTER. Why would you *prefer* to think I would be disloyal to the – to those who have *provided* for us? To those who – ?

SAMIRA. I don't know. I just do.

WALTER. To – ? I don't know what's gotten into you, but I've never been so confused about you in my life.

SAMIRA. Do you want me to help you with your homework?

WALTER. We're *ruined*!

SAMIRA. No. Because we know how to lie. I'll help you lie, and you'll win the test, and we'll keep the secret. If that's what you want. Is that what you want?

WALTER. Do I have a choice?

SAMIRA. Yes.

WALTER. No, I *don't* have a choice, actually. So yes, that's what I want.

SAMIRA. Really?

WALTER. Goddammit. You're killing me.

SAMIRA. No. Stop saying those things. I'm going to help you. What's your blue picture?

WALTER. Please. I…

SAMIRA. The cool blue picture. The blue "button." What is it?

WALTER. When we went back to Rabat. On our honeymoon. We went to the market, and it was so hot. Then we met your sister at the hotel bar, and I had a Guinness. It was warm, but I took a big swallow, and I said "Man, that hits the spot." "That's a good Guinness." Remember that?

SAMIRA. Yes.

WALTER. So, that's, that's it.

SAMIRA. The Guinness.

WALTER. Yes.

SAMIRA. That works for you?

WALTER. Well. Well, it was a good, it was a good moment.

SAMIRA. The *beer* you drank on our honeymoon.

WALTER. What's wrong with it?

SAMIRA. It's a drink that you had. You think it's going to, to *transform* you, in your mind?

WALTER. This is not, this kind of reflection, this is not something I claim to be good at.

SAMIRA. That's why I'm asking to help you. But what about me?

WALTER. What do you mean?

SAMIRA. You chose our honeymoon. But a drink? Not me? Don't *I* calm you?

WALTER. Yes, but. Yes, but, I need a specific *moment.* Something I can *narrow* my…

SAMIRA. *(thinking)* Hm.

WALTER. *Narrow* my…

SAMIRA. Yes.

WALTER. *Focus.*

SAMIRA. You went onto the, the place, the *veranda.* Later, when we went up to the room. It was late in the day, but it was still hot. I told you come in to the air conditioning, but you said you were just going to look out at the city for a bit. I came out with a bottle of water, very cold from the ice bucket. I put my cool hand on your shoulder, and you said "That feels good." So I put – I *pressed* the bottle to my lips, for a long…moment. Then I put my lips to the back of your neck. Held your chin in my hand and pressed your neck against my cool lips. And you said, "Ah, that's good."

WALTER. Right.

SAMIRA. Do you remember?

WALTER. Yeah. That could work.

SAMIRA. And your blue button will be here…on the back of your neck…where you can reach up and touch it…

WALTER. I won't be able to reach up…

SAMIRA. With your mind, then. Yes?

WALTER. Huh. Yes. Wow. You're good at this.

SAMIRA. Well. A compliment.

WALTER. Yeah. What do you mean?

SAMIRA. I can't remember the last compliment.

WALTER. I compliment you all the time.

SAMIRA. When was the last compliment?

WALTER. The – I said – I don't remember the *last* one, but I said, just the other day I said "You're too smart to be religious."

SAMIRA. Oh. That was a compliment?

WALTER. Of course. "You're too *smart.*" "*Smart.*" That's a compliment.

SAMIRA. Oh.

WALTER. To grow up as you did. In an Islamic culture. To turn your back on it. You – that's *heroic.* I mean, that's quite a *compliment,* right? To you.

SAMIRA. I said it could be good for children, maybe, to be raised in a spiritual household. If it teaches peace.

WALTER. And I said you're too smart for that.

SAMIRA. And "peace is bad."

WALTER. No. "Peace is overrated." Is what I said.

SAMIRA. It doesn't sound like a compliment.

WALTER. "Smart" is a compliment. What can I say? Now, please. I have to work on this. Don't you understand? This is the most important…*task* of my life.

SAMIRA. Yes. I understand. What is your red picture?

WALTER. It's supposed to be disturbing. Alarming. *Violent,* maybe. It has to increase my stress. My cardiovascular. Perspiration. Respiration.

SAMIRA. And you can't think of anything?

WALTER. No. I'm not good at this. It requires…

SAMIRA. Imagination?

WALTER. I don't have an "imagination," Samira?

SAMIRA. I'm not using the word correctly?

WALTER. The ability to…*conjure*…creative ideas, with the… *faculties* of the mind?

SAMIRA. Yes. I'm using it correctly.

WALTER. I don't *have* that. Is what you're saying.

SAMIRA. I don't always know what's an insult for you. I didn't know you *valued* this. I'm sorry.

WALTER. I have an imagination. Just not for things like this. Not for…

SAMIRA. Feelings.

(*off his look*)

Now what? I can't seem to say the right thing today. Let's just do the red picture.

(*coaxing*)

I thought it was important.

WALTER. It should be disturbing.

SAMIRA. Like a horror movie.

WALTER. Yes, but personal. It should be personally disturbing.

SAMIRA. Like death? People dying?

WALTER. Yes.

SAMIRA. The blacks in Rhodesia, maybe.

WALTER. What?

SAMIRA. The blacks in the townships. The ones who died of the anthrax.

Thousands of them were sick. Ten thousand? How many died? Hundreds?

You could picture all those bodies. Dead bodies, of people dead from the anthrax. That's disturbing.

(*pause*)

WALTER. I said it should be personal.

SAMIRA. It was your anthrax, wasn't it?

You made anthrax for the government. Those blacks were a problem. They got anthrax.

WALTER. You don't "make" anthrax.

SAMIRA. You know what I mean. "Weaponized."

WALTER. It was the Cold War. Those were rough times.

SAMIRA. And we *won* the Cold War. So it worked. *That's* good. So, is that why it's not a good red picture?

WALTER. What do you mean?

SAMIRA. The anthrax bodies. It's not good for a red picture, I see that. But is it because it's not personal, as you said?

WALTER. Yes.

SAMIRA. ...Or because it's not *distressing*. As you said.

WALTER. Of course it's distressing.

SAMIRA. But you said they had it coming.

WALTER. I didn't say they had it coming. I said it was the Cold War.

SAMIRA. And they were the enemy.

WALTER. Yes. But of course it's *distressing*.

SAMIRA. Because of the children.

WALTER. Because of the whole *thing*.

SAMIRA. But mostly because of the children, who didn't know it was the Cold War.

WALTER. Because of the whole *thing*, Samira.

SAMIRA. Because most of the *adults* probably didn't know it was the Cold War, either. Right?

WALTER. It's *distressing*, but it isn't *personal*. You see? It's been *decades*. I was a *boy*, practically. *Weeks* out of college. And it wasn't *personal*, because I didn't *see* piles of goddamn bodies. I didn't see one body. I did my job and I came home.

SAMIRA. *(helpfully)* Well, let's forget it, then.

WALTER. Yes.

SAMIRA. We'll think of something else.

WALTER. Who have you been talking to?

SAMIRA. Nobody.

WALTER. Because you sound – and don't deny it, because I can tell; I'm not *so* dense – You sound like you're judging me, all of a sudden, even though we've had these conversations before, and you've *never...* This is what's so bizarre: You've never had a problem with me before. In this respect. And now, my *God*, you've sent a fucking – *Holy* – You've sent a classified fucking memo to a goddamn civil *rights* group, to *ruin* me, to *ruin* me, and now you're taking a position on some thirty-year old shit in *Rhodesia*? That you *always* knew about, from practically Day Fucking One? And never had a problem with? Until *today*?

SAMIRA. *(dropping the act)* You should be ashamed of yourself, cursing at your wife like a, like a drunken sailor or something! And it wasn't today that I've changed! I've been changing for years and you apparently did not notice! I've been changing since the day you brought me to this country! And you haven't noticed!

WALTER. So, are you too good for me now, is that it?

SAMIRA. I'm *worried* for you. I have that much sense. I'm worried for when they ask you if you dislike black people, or just the ones you helped *kill*?!

WALTER. They're not going to *ask* that! And I don't dislike black people, anyway. *You* do. For God's sake, you said they were animals.

SAMIRA. And what did *you* say?

WALTER. I said you were *wrong*.

SAMIRA. No, you didn't. You said I went too *far*. Which is different. And then you married me.

WALTER. Because I was in love with you.

SAMIRA. You were in love with someone who said black people were animals.

WALTER. That's b– You're attacking me for loving you?

SAMIRA. No, I'm s– Oh, don't pretend to be sentimental to win a fight.

WALTER. I'm n– Huh?

SAMIRA. No, you should not have loved me.

WALTER. Look: Samira: I knew you were just an ignorant girl from North Africa who was just repeating things she heard around her. Okay?

SAMIRA. But even though I was so ignorant, you never tried to change my mind.

WALTER. Why? What difference did it make? I knew you were smart enough not to say it at *parties*.

SAMIRA. You never noticed when I changed.

WALTER. I noticed. And it's *fine*. But was I supposed to embarrass you with it? "Hey, I've noticed you're not such a racist anymore"? "Since you've been watching *Oprah*"?

SAMIRA. What if it *was* Oprah? So what? Is that supposed to make me silly? Because it was Oprah, and not…Mandela, or someone?

And I knew about Rhodesia from Day One because you *bragged* about it! And you may have been a boy when it happened, but you were a man when you bragged to me about it, because that was only ten years ago!

WALTER. I was not bragging, and I / have never brought it up…

SAMIRA. You *were* bragging. I know you. In that way where / "I can't say so much, because it's all very secret…"

WALTER. I was not bragging, and I have… No. I was not bragging, and I haven't brought it up since.

SAMIRA. Because you got a new job, and you knew they thought it would look bad, if people would find out! So you never mentioned it again, even to me, because that's how you make things go away! That's how you're going to pass this lie test – by making it all go away! The stupid Africans and the stupid memo and your stupid wife who watches Oprah! I'll tell you what your red picture should be: It should be me being *FUCKED* by black Africans who have the ANTHRAX!

(A knock at the door.)

WALTER. Oh shit. Please, Samira. I'm begging you.

(He opens the door, revealing **ROGER STANHOPE** *in the hallway.)*

/ Rog–

ROGER. Who's fucking *who*, now?

WALTER. Oh – *God*. She was just – Come in, will you?

(ROGER *enters.)*

Don't say "fucking" in the hallway.

ROGER. Oh. Sorry. Just…

WALTER. She was…making… / helping me with something.

ROGER. Sure. I know. Sorry. Hi, Samira. But why don't you get a *house*, like everyone else? Then we can say fucking this, and / fucking that…

WALTER. Yeah, she was – we were discussing something.

ROGER. Apparently.

WALTER. No. Ha.

ROGER. I'm just teasing you. But why not buy a house? It's the bloody suburbs. Do you have a gambling problem?

WALTER. No. We have enough room. We…

ROGER. Can I have a Coke or something? I'm parched.

WALTER. Sure, sure. Honey? No. I'll get it. Coke, or 7-Up, or…?

ROGER. Coke, please.

WALTER. We have beer.

ROGER. No. Coke, thanks. How are you, Samira?

SAMIRA. I'm fine.

ROGER. Bea was just saying how long it's been since we've had you to dinner.

SAMIRA. It's nice of her to think of us.

ROGER. When she's remodeled the kitchen, she'll want to show it off.

SAMIRA. That will be nice.

ROGER. Good. You know – I'm glad you're here. It occurs to me there's something I wanted to ask you.

SAMIRA. Oh?

ROGER. Yes. I was just wondering: Did you leak that confidential memo to Amnesty International? By any chance?

WALTER. *What*? Roger. *What* the *hell*?

ROGER. Come on, Walter. I'm just asking. Let's just ask the question.

SAMIRA. I don't know what you mean.

WALTER. *(to* **ROGER***)* See? What is wrong with you?

ROGER. *(to* **SAMIRA***)* You know the memo I mean, though.

SAMIRA. The one that was on the internet, I suppose.

WALTER. *(to* **ROGER***)* Why would you do that?

ROGER. I had to ask.

WALTER. Why? Why did you have to ask?

ROGER. I'm asking everyone.

WALTER. You're asking *everyone*. In hopes of what? That someone will say, "Oh, yes, that was me. Why do you ask?"

ROGER. You never know.

WALTER. That was ridiculous, Roger. Here's your Coke.

ROGER. Thank you.

WALTER. Is that why you wanted to come over here? / To ask her that?

ROGER. No, no, no. And yes. Yes and no. I *did* want to discuss our reaction to the… Our PR strategy, if you will, in light of the – *whatever. Yes.* I needed to ask her.

WALTER. I don't understand this.

ROGER. I'm just being vigilant.

SAMIRA. If I had done it, do you think I would just betray my husband to you, just like that?

ROGER. Mm. Possibly?

SAMIRA. I'm going out.

ROGER. Oh, no no. Please don't be offended.

SAMIRA. I'm not at all offended. I'm just going out.

WALTER. Where are you going?

SAMIRA. To Jennifer's. Where's my phone?

WALTER. I thought you were tired.

SAMIRA. I'm awake now. I feel like going out.

ROGER. I can't help feeling I've made you angry.

SAMIRA. Certainly not. You were right to ask. I'm happy to say that I would never, ever do such a thing.

WALTER. If you're just mad at Roger, he's…goddammit, he's leaving.

ROGER. I've just started my Coke.

SAMIRA. He can stay, Walter. I'm going out.

WALTER. I, I, I, I don't know *why* he would ask you that.

ROGER. You're making much too big a deal of it. Let's relax.

SAMIRA. Yes, dear. Please. You both have a lot to talk about. And none of it concerns me. In any way.

ROGER. Samira, it was so nice to see you again. We *will* have you to dinner. It's been too long.

SAMIRA. That sounds wonderful. And I'm so sorry you had to hear me yelling at my husband earlier.

WALTER. / Honey…

ROGER. "Yelling" at him? Surely not. If so, I'm sure he deserved it.

SAMIRA. Yes. It was about the two of you killing all those people in Rhodesia.

ROGER. Ahmm…

SAMIRA. Now, where did I put my…? / Ah.

ROGER. Shit. Well, that won't do.

(He raises his shirt to reveal a small recording device.)

Talk amongst yourselves, while I sort this out.

(He switches it off, and erases the recording.)

We can't just go back a few seconds; they'll hear the edit. We'll have to start the whole thing over.

WALTER. What is that?

ROGER. It's a recorder, obviously. The problem is, if I cut it off just before Samira's controversial allegation, they'll wonder why. They're very paranoid, right now, and they know we're friends.

WALTER. Roger.

ROGER. I can't bring them a five-minute recording, can I? Oh, close your mouth, will you? And I can't bring them something all chopped up. We've got to just go again.

(**WALTER** *looks stunned.*)

Walter.

WALTER. Roger. What...?

ROGER. Walter. We're *friends*. If anyone had said anything incriminating, I would have called it off.

WALTER. You're *recording* us?

ROGER. They didn't give me much of a choice. I mean, what would you have had me say? "No"? "That seems *wrong* to me, a bit"? The point is, I'm bringing you in on it.

WALTER. Because she said that...thing.

ROGER. What do you mean?

WALTER. You're only telling us about it because she said something you didn't want on the tape.

ROGER. Oh oh oh. Yes. Well. I didn't want to tell you *ahead* of time. The conversation wouldn't have been natural. I mean, you're not *actors*, either of you. But, obviously, we should have gone that route.

SAMIRA. Why would Chenoweth care if you killed some people in Rhodesia?

WALTER. Samira.

ROGER. Walter and I are part of the public face of the company. You see?

SAMIRA. Yes. He's mentioned that.

ROGER. Chenoweth can tolerate some rough types in the mix, of course – that's sort of the idea. But if they discovered that Walter and I had a history of, of *race relations*, well, they might think of that as too much of a...vulnerability.

SAMIRA. Because you might lose your…

ROGER. Right.

SAMIRA. Your government contracts.

ROGER. Precisely.

WALTER. You're recording our conversations for Chenoweth?

ROGER. Good God, *yes.* As I've explained.

WALTER. Is that even legal?

ROGER. No.

WALTER. You *asked* her if she leaked the memo!

ROGER. Of course. / I knew she…

WALTER. That thing was running.

ROGER. Yes. Because I knew she would deny it. Of course.

WALTER. You came in here wearing a *wire.*

ROGER. You're choosing to completely misunderstand the circumstances, simply because of / the sensational…

WALTER. You're wearing a *wire.*

ROGER. …The sensational nature of someone…

WALTER. Because you're / wearing a…

ROGER. Yes. Because of someone revealing a…

WALTER. Wearing a *wire.*

ROGER. …Revealing a recording device, in your…

WALTER. Get out of here.

ROGER. Wait, now. I'm trying to explain to you. I'm in a lot of trouble right now. We all are. I couldn't say no. But I knew, Walter, I knew you'd both make a clear, unequivocal denial. Which is perfect for everyone. I'm doing you a huge favor right now. Look, I could have skittered out of here, you know, skittered off, and you'd be none the wiser. But what have I done? I've *revealed* to you, the ruse. So that we can…

WALTER. Roger…

ROGER. So that we can use it to our advantage. But I can't go back with nothing. We have to make a new recording.

SAMIRA. Can I hear what I sounded like?

ROGER. I'm sorry, dear. I've already erased it.

SAMIRA. Oh.

ROGER. But we'll make a new one.

SAMIRA. No, thank you. I'm not an actress, as you say. I would probably forget my lines, and confess.

WALTER. Ha. She's kidding.

ROGER. Why would you confess to something you didn't do?

SAMIRA. Exactly.

ROGER. Exactly what?

SAMIRA. Exactly as Walter says. I'm kidding.

ROGER. You know I love you, Samira, but you absolutely cannot tell a joke.

SAMIRA. In French, I'm funny. In Arabic, I'm hilarious.

ROGER. Would you like to confess in Arabic? I speak a little.

WALTER. No. Shut up. I don't like the tone of this.

ROGER. The recorder's off. Look.

WALTER. I don't care. She didn't do it, and you know it.

ROGER. Of course.

WALTER. Yes. And that's it.

ROGER. Right. But I still have to bring back a recording.

WALTER. Tell them we weren't home.

ROGER. Well…

WALTER. What's wrong with that?

ROGER. Why not get it over with? It has to happen some time. It'll be good practice.

WALTER. For what?

ROGER. For your polygraph, for one thing.

WALTER. Why would I need to practice for my polygraph?

ROGER. Walter.

WALTER. What?

ROGER. For what *she* said.

WALTER. About what?

ROGER. Rhodesia. It'll come up.

WALTER. How can it come up?

ROGER. In a million ways. "Have you lied about your past?" "Have you lied to your employers?"

WALTER. Those would be *comparison* questions. I'm *supposed* to lie about those.

ROGER. I don't think they care what the questions are *called.* They're still embarrassing.

WALTER. They have to go over the questions ahead of time.

ROGER. Really?

WALTER. Yes.

ROGER. Um… You know that you're specifically prohibited from doing research on polygraphs. It's okay with me, of course, but…

WALTER. So why mention it?

ROGER. To caution you against, you know, sharing your research. As you're doing with me.

WALTER. Oh.

ROGER. Yes, but I'm honored. In fact, I'm encouraging you to, to do whatever. Just pass it, right? But pass it all. All the embarrassing questions. Do you see?

WALTER. I'm trying.

ROGER. You know what the Russians told Aldrich Ames, when he was facing the polygraph?

WALTER. What.

ROGER. "Just relax." That's it. That's all they said. And you know what?

WALTER. He passed.

ROGER. That's right.

SAMIRA. Who's Aldrich Ames?

ROGER. Oh, he sold some things to the bad guys. Now let's make this recording, and I'll be out of your way.

SAMIRA. I don't want to make a recording.

ROGER. You want to help Walter, don't you? Be a sport. Just say what you said before, and you can excuse yourself, or whatever. Okay?

SAMIRA. Is this what you want, Walter?

WALTER. Yeah, actually. This might be a good thing.

SAMIRA. Fine. Turn the thing on.

ROGER. We have to do the whole bit, or they'll be suspicious. I'll go out and knock.

WALTER. Okay.

(**ROGER** *exits, still holding his drink.*)

SAMIRA. Where should I be?

WALTER. Wherever. I don't think it matters.

(**ROGER** *knocks.* **WALTER** *immediately opens the door.*)

WALTER. Oh, hi, / Roger.

ROGER. Whoa. Well, well, hi, Walter, / you must have…

WALTER. Come in.

ROGER. You must have been right at the door. / Thank you.

WALTER. Hm?

ROGER. You must have – Hi, Samir–

(*dropping character*)

You can't be right at the door.

WALTER. Oh.

ROGER. You have to wait / a second or two.

WALTER. Sorry.

ROGER. Let's go again.

(*exits*)

WALTER. Sorry.

(*Closes door. Pause.* **ROGER** *knocks.* **WALTER** *waits, then opens door.*)

Oh. Hi, Roger.

ROGER. Well, hello.

WALTER. Come in.

ROGER. Thank you. Hello, Samira.

SAMIRA. Hello.

(**ROGER**, *quite audibly, tilts crushed ice into his mouth, with:*)

WALTER. Do you want something to drink?

(**ROGER** *spits out the ice.*)

ROGER. Shit. We've blown the take.

WALTER. Huh?

SAMIRA. This is too hard.

ROGER. No, no. We're just working out the kinks. Take four.

(Puts down the glass. Exits. Pause.)

SAMIRA. Maybe he left for good this time.

(Knock. Pause. **WALTER** *opens door.)*

WALTER. Oh, hi, Roger.

ROGER. Well, hello.

WALTER. Come in.

ROGER. Thank you. Hello, Samira.

SAMIRA. Hello.

ROGER. And how have you been?

SAMIRA. Fine.

WALTER. I'll get you a drink.

ROGER. Oh. Thank you. I'm parched. You two should get a house.

SAMIRA. We don't have children.

ROGER. Ah.

SAMIRA. I want to adopt.

ROGER. Oh. How nice. And how does Walter feel about that?

WALTER. It might be a good idea. She could use more help around the house.

ROGER. Ah. How, sort of, *Dickensian.*

SAMIRA. *(abruptly)* Why have you come here?

ROGER. Oh. To…well, I need to speak to Walter about some issues that have been / raised at…

WALTER. Your drink.

ROGER. Oh. A *Coke*. It's as if you read my mind.

WALTER. Right. I mean, um, is that okay?

ROGER. It's fine, thanks. But, now, you might as well know, Samira, since you ask: we're good friends, right? You would never lie to me about something…about something very serious.

SAMIRA. No. What is it?

ROGER. Well, now, I hope you won't be offended, but I have to ask you about this memo.

SAMIRA. What memo?

ROGER. Well. The one that was recently leaked to the media.

SAMIRA. Oh?

WALTER. *(tensely)* You know about the memo.

SAMIRA. No, I don't.

WALTER. *(glaring lasers into her)* Samira. You know about this memo. Everyone is *talking* about it. It was *released*. To the *media*.

SAMIRA. *(up to speed)* Yes. I would know about it from the media.

ROGER. Yes. So. My question is, did you happen to see it *before* it…it…went *out*.

SAMIRA. What did it say?

WALTER. Well, honey, you wouldn't have seen *any* memo, from my work, would you? I wouldn't – Look, Roger, I hope you're not suggesting that I would ever, *ever* bring home anything from work that I would put in the way of my wife or anyone else, for God's sake. I mean, come *on*. What are you accusing me of?

ROGER. I'm sorry, pal, / I just felt I had to…

WALTER. And my *wife*. What do you think we are? How could you even *ask* an idiotic question like that?

ROGER. / Well, I…

WALTER. You should be *ashamed* of yourself. You know me better than that.

ROGER. I just had to ask. I'm sorry.

WALTER. I think you should leave now.

ROGER. Yes.

(He starts to go.)

SAMIRA. What did it say, though?

ROGER. / Huh?

WALTER. Honey…

SAMIRA. This memo. I don't really follow these things. But some Nigerians. They were found dead, recently? Is that right?

WALTER. It's ridiculous.

(He gestures for **ROGER** *to leave.* **ROGER** *ignores him.)*

ROGER. Some criminals were found dead, yes.

SAMIRA. Protesters. Yes?

ROGER. Vandals. Our lab in Nigeria was vandalized, and then these locals showed up dead, and some idiot, / some…

SAMIRA. Shot in the back of their heads.

ROGER. Yes. Shot in the back of their heads.

SAMIRA. And left in a ditch. Yes?

ROGER. Yes. Left in a ditch.

SAMIRA. And "some idiot"…?

ROGER. Yes. This…ha!…this Human Resources *cretin*, this *imbecile*, actually took it upon himself to recommend a, what do you call it, a psychological *review* of the boys who are *alleged* to have done it.

SAMIRA. Post-traumatic…

ROGER. Yes! Post-traumatic stress disorder! For Security personnel! And then, good God: He CC'd it to every Science Department! For its scientific interest!

(laughs, then stops)

Which doesn't mean we did it.

SAMIRA. It doesn't?

ROGER. Of course not. It just means he's an idiot with an e-mail account and his head up his arse all day.

SAMIRA. But it sure looks bad.

ROGER. Don't worry, Samira. We'll be all right.

SAMIRA. Will Walter be all right?

ROGER. / Of course.

WALTER. Honey, it's fine. It isn't relevant. Should we…

(He gestures "turn it off" to **ROGER**, *who returns an "it's okay" wave.)*

SAMIRA. It isn't relevant?

WALTER. To this conversation.

ROGER. Or at all. Even if the allegation were true, which it isn't, it wouldn't even be against the law.

SAMIRA. Really?

WALTER. *("on topic")* The point is, we had nothing to do with that memo, and that's it.

ROGER. *(to* **SAMIRA***)* We're independent contractors, in a foreign land. U.S. laws do not apply to us, and if our hosts have a problem with us, they'll ask us to leave. Which they haven't.

SAMIRA. Because they need the money.

ROGER. We're not responsible for the problems they've created for themselves. It's like the bloody wild west down there.

WALTER. But we had nothing to do with the memo being leaked, and that's… / that's the thing.

ROGER. They're creating their own hell down there. What can we do?

WALTER. Exactly. So that's it.

SAMIRA. I remember a story I heard once.

WALTER. Honey, he needs to go.

(He gives her a broad "wrap it up" gesture, which she ignores.)

SAMIRA. There was this king, in this kingdom, and he had this huge catapult. This enormous catapult, that he was very proud of.

ROGER. This would have been a long time ago.

SAMIRA. Yes. And when a citizen was unhappy, and would complain, the king would say, "You should go to another country," and then he would put the person in the catapult, and *fling* him over the trees, into the next country.

ROGER. I imagine that put an end to the whining.

SAMIRA. But no, it didn't. People kept complaining, and the king kept shooting them in the catapult, to the next country. Day after day, month after month, many people.

ROGER. Hm.

SAMIRA. Then, finally, one day, some people came from the other country, to see the king. And they said, "You must stop this. How can you kill all these people?" And the king said, "*Kill* them? You mean you haven't been *catching* them?"

(pause)

ROGER. As I said, darling, you cannot tell a joke.

SAMIRA. It wasn't funny?

WALTER. So, anyway. *There.* We didn't do it. You should go now, Roger.

ROGER. Of course. Thanks for the beverage. Sorry to have bothered you. See you at the office.

(He gives them a wink and a thumbs up, and exits. Pause.)

SAMIRA. How did I do?

(blackout)

End of Scene

Scene Three

(**PEOPLES**' *office.* **WALTER** *is sitting in the polygraph chair, facing out.* **PEOPLES** *is hooking him up to the computerized machine.*)

PEOPLES. You got a movement sensor under your behind. You try to flex them cheeks and it's gonna make a peak on my chart, and then I've caught you using CM, you understand?

WALTER. Yes.

PEOPLES. You do?

WALTER. Yes.

PEOPLES. You know what CM means?

WALTER. Of course.

PEOPLES. No, you do not.

WALTER. It means countermeasures.

PEOPLES. How do you know that?

WALTER. How do I – ? I've been studying this all week.

PEOPLES. No, you dang well have *not* been studying this. At *all.* You understand me?

WALTER. I see.

PEOPLES. That was your first test. Somebody says "CM" and you say, "Oh. Countermeasures," and they've *got* you. They know you / been studying.

WALTER. Right. I get it. / I – I –

PEOPLES. You got to watch out.

WALTER. Right. I didn't know you were…in character, / or whatever.

PEOPLES. This is rehearsal. You can't make assumptions.

WALTER. Okay.

PEOPLES. These are pneumograph traces. They measure your respiration. Are those too tight?

WALTER. No.

PEOPLES. No matter what else you mighta read, don't try to fake your breathing.

WALTER. Hm.

PEOPLES. You can't know how *hard* to breathe, how long to *hold* it, it won't conform to the other graphs, it'll just look erratic. You understand me?

WALTER. Umm…

PEOPLES. What.

WALTER. See, I don't know if you're testing me now, / or…

PEOPLES. No no. I'm trying to tell you something.

WALTER. You should give me some sort of signal, or / something.

PEOPLES. No, I'm not testing y– How I'm gonna give you a signal, if I'm testing you?

WALTER. You could just say, "From now on, I'm pretending / to be.."

PEOPLES. No, no. It – It's not that big a deal. / These are…

WALTER. You could touch your nose with your finger, or…

PEOPLES. If I – What do you mean, touch my nose?

WALTER. Like…

(demonstrates)

PEOPLES. We don't need to do that.

WALTER. We'll see.

PEOPLES. It will all be clear to you. Now, I was saying: these are electrodermal sensors, measure your skin conductivity. Keep your hands still. Comfortable?

WALTER. I guess.

PEOPLES. This cuff measures your cardiovascular activity. Blood pressure. I'm gonna pump it up, now. How's that feel?

WALTER. Okay.

PEOPLES. Good. Now just relax.

(He sits at the desk, just out of **WALTER***'s periphery. Makes a few clicks on the laptop, and studies the screen.)*

Here we go.

Is your name Walter Krootzer?

WALTER. Kreutzer. Yes.

(There is a 15-second pause after every answer.)

PEOPLES. Are we in the United States of America?

WALTER. Yes.

PEOPLES. Have you ever violated your own code of ethics?

WALTER. No.

PEOPLES. Have you ever brought a confidential memo home from work?

WALTER. No.

PEOPLES. Are we sitting outdoors?

WALTER. No.

PEOPLES. Have you ever lied to your supervisors about anything?

WALTER. No.

PEOPLES. Did you show a confidential memo to your wife?

WALTER. No.

PEOPLES. Did you ever say the holocaust was exaggerated?

WALTER. What?

PEOPLES. Did you ever tell a bunch of white supremacists that the holocaust was an exaggeration?

WALTER. *(rattled)* That isn't one of the questions.

PEOPLES. Did you?

WALTER. This is not a question that we discussed! They're not going to ask a question that wasn't discussed ahead of time. That's not how it works.

PEOPLES. Well, "surprise" then, I guess. You don't know *what* they might do.

WALTER. There's *no* test… There's *no* test that uses surprise questions.

PEOPLES. Maybe I'm some crazy cowboy, runnin' off on his own, no respect for the guidelines of the American Polygraph Association.

WALTER. You have to stick to the questions!

PEOPLES. I don't have to do diddly-nothin', except discover your mendacious propensities by any means I choose.

WALTER. Wait a minute. Are you supposed to be in character?

PEOPLES. Huh?

WALTER. Are you speaking / for yourself, or preten–

PEOPLES. Yes. No, I'm pretending to be the examiner, Walt. You know how this works.

WALTER. I want you to stop…checking *up* on me! Just stop…running / checks on me!

(He tries to extricate himself.)

PEOPLES. Be careful with that equipment.

WALTER. Get me out of here. / Just – Just –

PEOPLES. Whoa, whoa. Don't pull on that stuff. You're gonna mess that up.

WALTER. I want my money back.

PEOPLES. Pardon me?

WALTER. You heard me.

PEOPLES. I'm not giving you your money back. I've put a lot of time into this, and I've shared my secrets with you. / Now, just sit still.

WALTER. Your secrets are worthless. Blue buttons, and red buttons…
/ *White…*

PEOPLES. Red Buttons? Remember him?

WALTER. What?

PEOPLES. Red *Buttons.* I never made that association before.

WALTER. I don't know what you're talking about. Just unhook me. Now.

PEOPLES. You don't think this'll work? You never lied to yourself before? 'Cause that's all you're doing.

WALTER. You're trying to…

PEOPLES. What.

WALTER. You're trying to fuck me.

PEOPLES. Whoa, hold on. Now, why would I do that?

WALTER. You know why.

PEOPLES. No, I don't. You paid me cash. To do what I do. This is what I do. Why would I want to undermine my livelihood?

WALTER. Because you don't like me.

PEOPLES. Walt. Hm. Walt. Were you pushing your buttons just now? During the test?

WALTER. Yes.

(**PEOPLES** *turns the laptop so* **WALTER** *can see it.*)

PEOPLES. Look how you freaked out, here, when I mentioned that holocaust business. You see that? You got all flustered, forgot how to lie to yourself. See?

WALTER. Yeah.

PEOPLES. But look here: The other questions. Your baseline is high and steady. Your relevant responses are shaky – I guess I'd have to give you a DI, but I'd puzzle over it first. It's that close. And we're just getting started. So, now, you don't have to care if I "like" you or not. You only have to understand that I'm your *friend*. Your *friend* did this for you, Walt.

WALTER. I'm not paying you to do research on me.

PEOPLES. I'm done with that. I just needed something to work with. That's all. We gotta rehearse everything. We even gotta rehearse the surprises. You want to be good at this, don't you?

WALTER. Yes.

PEOPLES. Then trust me.

WALTER. We're supposed to be working on the Comparison model. Comparison Test doesn't have surprises.

PEOPLES. Walter, you ain't trying to get a job at Office Depot. You are a scientist at a defense business. You think they're not gonna assume you studied this stuff? They are going to seek to mess you up. They're gonna attack you on the pre-test. They're gonna attack you on the test. They're gonna attack you on the post-test. You know why? Because they're mercenaries. We got an adjective for them: *mercenary*.

WALTER. If they really believe I'm guilty, they'll get me.

PEOPLES. I'm gonna change your attitude. Today. Right now. Now, straighten up. Shake it off. Relax. We're gonna go again.

(He returns to the desk.)

Now, this time, really push them red buttons. Now I can't say it without thinking "Red Buttons." Remember him? Never got a dinner?

That's alright. You ready?

WALTER. Yeah.

PEOPLES. Here we go: Is your name Walter Krootzer?

WALTER. Kreutzer. Yes.

PEOPLES. Did you say the holocaust was exaggerated?

WALTER. God DAMN it!

PEOPLES. *(innocent)* You didn't think I was / gonna ask it?

WALTER. Son of a BITCH!

PEOPLES. I didn't say I wasn't gonna / ask it.

WALTER. It was the *second* fucking *question*!

PEOPLES. It's my Sacrifice Relevant.

WALTER. That's not a Sacrifice Relevant. That's not a Sacrifice fucking / Relevant!

PEOPLES. Walter. Walter.

WALTER. *What.*

PEOPLES. My niece can probably hear you out there.

WALTER. Listen to me: They were a *paying* audience. It was a business arrangement. I'm a *scientist.* If someone wants to know the facts about something, I, I, I – It's an obligation. It's practically an *obligation.*

PEOPLES. You're totally messing up this chart, Walt.

WALTER. Do you hear me?

PEOPLES. Yeah. What were the facts?

WALTER. The f– They wanted to hear about Leuchter's study of, of Zyklon B residue at Auschwitz. It's a bullshit study, and I as much as said so.

PEOPLES. This chart says you're lying.

WALTER. Goddammit, are you watching the chart?

PEOPLES. I'm just telling you…

WALTER. I thought "only the examiner" could tell I was lying.

PEOPLES. Well, he's looking at this chart, and he says you're lying.

WALTER. You can't use it that way.

PEOPLES. You gotta stop thinking about how I can use it. I am beholden to no one. Now, you're saying you went all that way to disappoint these people?

WALTER. I told them it was inconclusive, alright? Which is true. Okay?

PEOPLES. Your cardiovascular is all over / the place.

WALTER. Of *course* my cardiovascular is all over the place. D'avore. What do you *think*?

PEOPLES. I'm just trying to get you to calm down.

WALTER. No, you *should* be trying to get me to calm down, but you're actually trying to get me *upset*. For some reason. I mean, what are you *doing* to me?

PEOPLES. I'm helping you.

WALTER. You are not helping me.

PEOPLES. So, you have – and I'm just asking out of curiosity – you have some sort of ethical, uh, *principle*, by which you are obligated to speak to anyone who pays you?

WALTER. As long as I don't *lie*, D'avore. Then, yes. As long as they understand that I'm bringing objective, factual…

PEOPLES. Yeah?

WALTER. Information, then…then…

PEOPLES. It's factual that the holocaust was exaggerated?

WALTER. Oh – Look. *Look*:

PEOPLES. Yeah?

WALTER. Why did they have to say six million?! That's all. Why not *four*? Isn't four enough?! Four and a half! Why *six*?! "Three to six million," they could say. Even that! I mean, I'm a scientist, that's all. Numbers *mean* something to me. To settle on the highest…possible…?

PEOPLES. What difference does it make?

WALTER. That's what I'm saying. That's my point. It's millions. We concede that it's millions. Why do we, why do we have to be held to this…this…

PEOPLES. Who's "we"?

WALTER. What do you mean?

PEOPLES. Who's "we"? You say "we" concede that it's millions.

WALTER. I mean "everyone."

PEOPLES. And why "concede"? Like you're in an argument about it. Why not just "say"? "Say" it's four million, or whatever. "Concede" sounds like you don't want to say it. Like you're reluctant. Right? If I understand that word.

WALTER. I'm not what you think I am.

PEOPLES. Okay.

WALTER. Those people are idiots. I understand that. I just – I just – I have to make a living.

PEOPLES. *(studying laptop screen)* Magic Eight Ball says "Yes." You have to make a living.

WALTER. Please stop pretending that you have any legitimate scientific basis for reading that thing right now.

PEOPLES. But you're not a history expert, are you?

WALTER. I'm a scientist. Statistics is a science.

PEOPLES. But you're not a statistics scientist, are you? You're a micro…botanist… / or…

WALTER. "Biologist."

PEOPLES. What I'm saying is, if *my* Klan meeting was looking for a speaker…

WALTER. It wasn't a Klan meeting.

PEOPLES. No, I'm saying…

WALTER. And they didn't call themselves white supremacists. If they had called themselves something, I wouldn't have gone.

PEOPLES. They didn't *call* themselves nothin'?

WALTER. They were the Truth In…Public…Something Society, or some bullshit.

PEOPLES. So I'm saying if my Truth Society was having a meeting, I'd hire a speaker I knew was, you know, sympathetic.

WALTER. I never professed sympathy. *Please.* I had some experiences in Rhodesia – interesting…political… These were eventful, complicated times. / Look…

PEOPLES. Rhodesia?

WALTER. Zimbabwe. It's Zimbabwe now.

PEOPLES. They got a lot of Jews down there? In Zimbabwe?

WALTER. No. Please. These were racial conflicts I had nothing to do with. Except I happened to be there at the time. That's all.

PEOPLES. So, black folks and white folks.

WALTER. Yes.

PEOPLES. Which side was the Truth Society on?

WALTER. Okay, that's it. Unhook me, or I'll do it myself. I'm done here. Keep the money, but I'm done with you.

PEOPLES. Hold on, Walter. Why you taking this so personal?

WALTER. You've *made* it personally. Personal. *You* have. You've got some kind of problem with me, and you're gonna waste the whole afternoon *interrogating* me about every little… / every little…

PEOPLES. *They* are going to interrogate you.

WALTER. Not about *this* stuff. Not about this. You think they care? You know what kind of people they have working there?

PEOPLES. What kind?

WALTER. Well. *All* kinds. All, different kinds. Is all I'm saying.

PEOPLES. I try not to judge people, Walter. Everybody's got a story, you know?

WALTER. Um. I could take that two ways.

PEOPLES. I don't follow.

WALTER. People say "Everybody's got a story," to *dismiss* that story. See? But, but…

PEOPLES. Huh?

WALTER. Sometimes people have an actual, *actual story…*

PEOPLES. Hmm. But my / point is…

WALTER. Worthy of acknowledgement. Some sort of…

PEOPLES. My point…

WALTER. …the benefit of the *doubt…*

PEOPLES. My point, Walter, my point is, if you don't get / your head together…

WALTER. The benefit of the *doubt.* My head? Just leave my fucking head out of it, okay? Just get out of my fucking head completely. Just do your fucking *job*, okay?

PEOPLES. I'm gonna urge you not to take that tone with me.

WALTER. *(redirecting his frustration) God.* I'm sorry. I'm *sorry.* Please. Can we – This is not – This / is not…

PEOPLES. Push that blue button.

WALTER. I can't.

PEOPLES. Push the blue button, now. Make these lines go down. Push it.

WALTER. I'm trying. But I don't believe in you.

PEOPLES. Walter…

WALTER. Wait.

(goes to his "blue" image)

PEOPLES. That's it. You're makin' it happen.

WALTER. You can't – You don't know.

PEOPLES. No no. Hold it down.

WALTER. *(getting agitated)* I have something in my head. An insect in my brain.

PEOPLES. What?

WALTER. I mean…

PEOPLES. You have a / insect in your…?

WALTER. That's not what I meant. I – That's not what I meant.

PEOPLES. / But you s–

WALTER. I was speaking metaphorically.

PEOPLES. *(warily)* Okay. Let's try to get back to zero. Just look at that white image. Look at that blank page.

WALTER. Okay.

PEOPLES. You see that blank, white page?

WALTER. Yes.

PEOPLES. You see it?

WALTER. Yes.

PEOPLES. There ain't a *insect* on it, is there?

WALTER. Goddammit, / I'm not crazy.

PEOPLES. Alright, / calm down.

WALTER. I'm not crazy. / Don't talk to me like I'm crazy.

PEOPLES. I know you're not. I know. I won't. Just relax.

WALTER. That's what they told Aldrich Ames, you know. Just relax. None of this bullshit, these blue pictures and / red pictures…

PEOPLES. He was probably a sociopath. You ain't a socio-path, *are* you.

WALTER. *You* would think so. *Wouldn't* you, D'avore? *You* would goddamn well think so.
   / *Wouldn't* you?

PEOPLES. No, I wouldn't think so. You want some water, or something?

WALTER. You *experts* don't know what you're talking about.

PEOPLES. That's what I'm sayin', Walt. That's why you gotta beat it by its own rules. Hedge your bets. If you gotta play poker with a guy who's cheating, you gotta cheat him yourself if you want to win. See? You just gotta keep telling yourself, over and over, the machine doesn't know, the machine is flawed, the machine doesn't know. We just want to catch liars, Walt. We all want to do something human beings ain't supposed to do. That's the only reason we keep using this piece of junk. It's all we got. We just want it so bad.

WALTER. You're wrong. You don't know if it works, because you don't *understand* it. You don't get it. I say, respectfully.

PEOPLES. Let me see these lines go down. Make 'em go down.

That's good. What don't I get?

WALTER. It isn't the examiner, it's the machine! You think the machine is flawed, but it isn't. It measures the observable truth. It's perfect. If it says you're lying, you're lying, even if you're telling the truth. If it says you're telling the truth, you *are*, even if you're lying. The machine is perfect. It's perfect. It's perfect. It's perfect.

PEOPLES. Walter.

WALTER. You're either lying or you're not, but you don't know until the machine tells you!

PEOPLES. *(skeptical)* I don't know about that.

WALTER. It's Schrödinger's cat. The observer's paradox.

PEOPLES. Are you seeing a cat here, now, Walter?

WALTER. No, I'm not seeing a *cat*. Schrödinger's cat. You put a cat in a radioactive box with a vial of hydrocyanic acid.

PEOPLES. Push those lines down.

That's good.

WALTER. It either killed the cat or it didn't. You don't know, until you, until you open the box and see. Until then, the cat is neither dead, nor alive. It's neither. It's both. At the same time. Until you open the box.

PEOPLES. *What's* the cat's name?

WALTER. *Schrödinger's* cat.

And *no*, I don't know the *cat's* name.

PEOPLES. Oh. Well, I really don't think that's how a polygraph works and also that's a terrible thing to do to a cat.

Are you pushing that blue button?

WALTER. Yes.

PEOPLES. That's fine. That's good.

Is your name Walter Krootzer?

WALTER. Kreutzer. Yes.

PEOPLES. Are we in the United States of America?

WALTER. Yes.

PEOPLES. Do you work for people who shoot folks in the head and throw them in a ditch like some garbage or something?

WALTER. No.

PEOPLES. Yeah, you're gonna be just fine, Walter. You're gonna be just fine.

(blackout)

End of Scene

Scene Four

(The condo. **SAMIRA** *is packing a large suitcase. She finishes packing, puts the suitcase in the middle of the floor, and sits. She hears* **WALTER** *off, jangling keys. She suddenly changes her plan, drags the suitcase out of sight.* **WALTER** *enters.)*

WALTER. Honey?

*(***SAMIRA** *enters.)*

WALTER. How was *your* day?

SAMIRA. How was yours?

WALTER. I need a better red picture. They only last so long, and then I need a new one.

I'm wearing them *out*, I guess. From practicing. All day, every day.

SAMIRA. All day, every day?

WALTER. That's what he said. Practice all day, every day.

SAMIRA. Red pictures, all day, every day?

What red pictures?

WALTER. They're unpleasant.

(pause)

SAMIRA. What red picture?

WALTER. To say it out loud. It's uncomfortable.

SAMIRA. What is it?

WALTER. Well. It's me…strangling you.

I told you it was unpleasant.

SAMIRA. Strangling me.

WALTER. You said I should use *you.* I'm taking your advice.

SAMIRA. But strangling me, it's losing its power?

WALTER. Samira, it's been a very long day. Please don't start picking at me again.

SAMIRA. No, but you have my eyes bugging out? My face turning purple? My tongue sticking out?

WALTER. You said to use you.

SAMIRA. No, I'm just checking. Checking your work. My tongue hanging out, I'm saying, "Please, Walter, no."

WALTER. You wouldn't be saying anything. You wouldn't be able to talk.

SAMIRA. Making strangled sounds, then. But you have the whole picture?

WALTER. Yes.

SAMIRA. But it doesn't *disturb* you enough.

WALTER. Don't put significance to it. It probably just isn't personal enough. It isn't from real life.

SAMIRA. Are you thinking you should really strangle me?

WALTER. Of course not.

SAMIRA. I'm not *inviting* you to strangle me. I'm only asking.

WALTER. I'm not going to strangle you. Don't worry. I just need something more real.

SAMIRA. You could imagine me leaving you.

WALTER. *(skeptical)* What would *that* look like?

SAMIRA. Me. Walking out the door. With a big suitcase.

WALTER. That doesn't really...hit the target. We can do better than that.

SAMIRA. No. That's the best I can do.

WALTER. I'm never gonna sleep tonight. I don't know what I'm gonna do.

SAMIRA. You could tell them enough is enough. You could tell them, I'm not going to put it in my brain that I'm strangling my lovely wife so I can keep working for killers. You could say, I copied that memo and I brought it home because I *wanted* to send it out for everyone to see. But I was too scared or, or confused, so my wife did it for me, out of love. To save me.

WALTER. I'm not going to say that, Samira. But thank you, anyway.

SAMIRA. I never wanted to leave you when you were so confused in your head. It seemed wrong. But I had to remind myself that you brought it on yourself. And now you're worse, with all these, all this...trying to make lying into truth, and truth into lying. I tried to help you. But I'm going.

(He finally realizes what she's telling him.)

WALTER. You *never* tried to help me. *Never.*

SAMIRA. Walter, do you love me?

WALTER. Yes.

SAMIRA. Then I'm going to leave you and maybe the pain will make you better.

WALTER. *(angling)* What if I *don't* love you?

SAMIRA. Then I'm going to leave you, and that's all.

WALTER. So, now that you've *ruined* my life. *Ruined* my life. Now that your work is done, now you're going to *leave* me!

SAMIRA. Yes. I don't like you.

WALTER. After all I've done for you?! Took you off that god-forsaken continent, gave you a real life? A life you couldn't have fucking *dreamed* of...?!

SAMIRA. Yes. I'm sorry about that. I'm going to go now.

WALTER. This was all *planned*, wasn't it? Oh, my God. You're a fucking... Tell me the truth. Just tell me the truth, now: are you in a cell, a sleeper cell, are you in a *sleeper cell*? I'm just asking, because if you are...Are you a *plant*? Some kind of...have you been working on this for *years*? It's not impossible, you know, don't look at me like it's fucking *impossible*! If your work here is done, if it's back to your friends...your *cell*...I'm entitled to ask! As your husband, as an innocent, fucking... I'm perfectly entitled to *ASK* THIS! I mean...oh my god, let me ask this, let me just *ask* you this, my god, just to *ask*: Did you figure how to get some anthrax, how to weaponize it, how to get your friends in to get some anthrax...? Fine. Fucking *look* at me like that. Go ahead. It's just how you would fucking look at me if you did it, too! And you know I'm right to ask. You know I'm right. Tell me. You've been...you've been...?

SAMIRA. What "friends," Walter?

WALTER. Tell me. Tell me the truth, now.

SAMIRA. What friends? Kim and Jennifer from Pilates? Those friends?

WALTER. If it isn't true, say so. If I'm wrong, just say so. You see how it looks.

SAMIRA. How it *looks*? How it *looks*?! How it looks to *you*, you crazy paranoid?! It looks fine to have an Arab wife when she obeys you! But when she leaves you, she must be a terrorist! I don't care if you're crazy, I won't let you be *this* crazy! / I won't stand for it!

WALTER. Maybe. Maybe. Okay. Maybe. On the other hand, that's just what they would *tell* you to say.

SAMIRA. You're *right*. And now I must *kill* you.

(She gets a paring knife from the kitchen, advances on him.)

I'm going to stab you with this knife, because that's what crazy fucking Arabs do. I'm going to cut you like I'm a crazy fucking Arab!

WALTER. Calm down. Alright. Calm down.

(She ululates, briefly.)

Okay. That's enough.

SAMIRA. *No*, Walter. I'm doing this for *you*. I see a perfect red picture for you now! The fear of it, the terrible *terror* of it will be your perfect red picture, when some crazy person came over from Africa and stabbed you in the chest with a *knife*!

WALTER. Samira, put it down.

SAMIRA. No, I'm serious! I'm giving you this gift! This perfect red picture! Your red button will be HERE, over your heart! Over your BLACK HEART!

WALTER. Samira.

SAMIRA. Yes, Walter?

WALTER. I can't have an injury at the examination. They'll think I'm using it as a countermeasure.

(*She stabs him in the chest.*)

OW! Shit! Oh my God! Don't pull it out! Don't pull it out! Let go!

(*She does. The knife protrudes from high in his left pectoral.*)

Shit. Call someone. Call nine-one-one. No. Call Roger. No. Shit. Don't call anyone.

(*Actually, she hasn't moved.*)

Don't call anyone.

How could you do this? How could you do this to me?

(*She retrieves the large suitcase, and also a couple of shoulder bags. She's loaded down.*)

Oh, my God. Oh, my God.

SAMIRA. Could you get the door?

WALTER. Could I get the *door*? I'm stabbed.

SAMIRA. You have two hands.

WALTER. I'm a little preoccupied, because you stabbed me.

(*She starts for the door.*)

No.

(*She stops.*)

No. No, Samira.

(*She opens the door.*)

SAMIRA. The morning after you brought home the memo, you were leaving for work. You were standing at this door, and you kissed me, and took my hand, and looked me in the eyes, and then you nodded, very slightly, you nodded your head without a word and I knew what it meant: it meant "send that memo because I cannot." And then you left without a word.

WALTER. I *nodded*? I NODDED? This is all because I nodded my head? You idiot! Are you completely out of your fucking MIND?

SAMIRA. *(calmly)* Oui. Je suis une folle. Au revoir et bonne chance.

(She exits.)

(He stands there, the knife protruding from his chest.)

(blackout)

End of Scene

Scene Five

(A small office in a research facility. There is a desk covered with computer equipment, a couple of chairs, a large cabinet – and there is a Medical NIR imaging array off to the side, and a video camera on a tripod.)

(ROGER *sits comfortably, his briefcase on the floor nearby, some documents on his lap. He's been hanging out here for a while. Right now, he's talking on his cell phone.)*

ROGER. Have you ever betrayed a friend? Have you ever –
Yes it is.

No, I don't think that will be necessary. I'm sure your guys have better things to do, anyway. He w–

Hm. I –

I say, he will proceed lamb-like…to the –

I'm sure.

No, it's like the Wing That Time Forgot over here. I'd think the place was abandoned, except for the occasional screams from behind the locked doors.

Yes, I *am* kidding. It was a joke.

Not yet. Just the polygraph.

I don't know; he's not out yet.

We'll get it. We'll get it after the fact. He'll confess.

Of *course* he'll go to the media; *everybody* goes to the media. But he'll have no Q-Rating. He's unpleasant. He'll be disliked. And the Arab wife, even more so.

Of course, *my* history has been expunged. You've seen to that, have you?

I should hope so.

(voices off)

Hold on, he might be coming.

No, don't bother sending anyone yet. I'll call you when we're getting close.

(WALTER *appears in the doorway.)*

WALTER. *(to someone offstage)* In here?

DR. DOLL. *(offstage)* If you / don't mind.

WALTER. *(notices* **ROGER***)* Oh. / They moved you –

ROGER. *(on phone)* That's… Mmhm. Okay. Okay. Yes. It's just as I told you.

No, the other thing I told you.

Yeah. I should go. I will. Goodbye.

(hangs up)

How are you?

WALTER. Okay. They moved you in here, huh?

ROGER. It's a delightful little room, isn't it?

WALTER. Roger, thank you so much for hanging around.

ROGER. Not at all. It's nice to get out of the lab, catch up on my homework. Did you know Somalia has become *dangerous* since we left? Says so right here.

(He tosses the document aside.)

(WALTER *sits, stiffly.)*

WALTER. I think I did well in there.

ROGER. I'm sure you did. How's that shoulder?

WALTER. Um. Okay. I hope I didn't tear a tendon or something.

ROGER. You should always stretch before engaging in vigorous activity. I've heard.

WALTER. I guess I need to improve my backhand. Why are we doing the post in here?

ROGER. The "post"?

WALTER. The "post-exam," or something, / I guess they call it.

ROGER. Oh. I guess we'll wait for Dr. Doll to tell us that.

WALTER. Why do they have an R&D guy doing polygraphs, anyway?

ROGER. It does seem odd. Maybe we should, uh… *Ah. Here* he comes.

(DR. DOLL *enters, holding a printout.)*

DR. DOLL. Okay. Well, Doctor? You feel good about that?

WALTER. Yes.

DR. DOLL. Well, it was NDI.

(pause)

WALTER. "NDI"?

DR. DOLL. You don't know what NDI means?

WALTER. No.

DR. DOLL. Ha. Okay. Well, it means No Deception Indicated.

WALTER. So I passed.

DR. DOLL. You passed.

WALTER. Fantastic. I can't wait to go thank my, uh, my superiors, for the opportunity to, uh, to waste my fucking time with this, this humiliating bullshit. Next time, I'm getting a lawyer, I don't care what anybody says, I'm getting a lawyer, because, because to have my loyalty questioned like this, to have my loyalty *questioned…*

ROGER. It's understandable. You're absolutely right.

WALTER. And you can put that on tape, Roger. I don't even care. It's / humiliating.

ROGER. We'll put it on tape later.

WALTER. So can I go, then? Is that it?

DR. DOLL. Not exactly.

WALTER. Not exactly? Well, what is it? What more do you want?

DR. DOLL. We still have Phase Two, unfortunately. Actually, *not* unfortunately. I am *enthusiastically* looking forward to Phase Two. Take your seat. This actually won't take long.

(DR. DOLL *goes to a cabinet, removes a wig-head on which is a Velcroed headband studded with diodes. He begins connecting it to the computer.)*

WALTER. But you said I passed. N…NDI, you said. That means I passed.

DR. DOLL. Phase One.

WALTER. Phase One? Nobody said anything about Phase One.

DR. DOLL. Oh. Okay: "That was Phase One."

WALTER. Roger, did you know about this?

ROGER. It rings a bell.

WALTER. It r– It – Roger?

ROGER. It'll be fine, Walter.

DR. DOLL. Doctor, I can't tell you how happy I am that you passed the polygraph. We've never had a subject who passed the polygraph and then failed the brain scan. You're going to prove this thing for us. Assuming you're guilty, of course.

WALTER. I'm not guilty.

DR. DOLL. No. Sure. That's great. But, you know, feel free to utilize countermeasures anyway. Seriously, that would make it even better. Step on a tack, bite your tongue, do math problems in your head, flex that racquetball injury – That's oozing a little, by the way; that must have been some match. Whatever you want. Seriously. I would love it. The point is, you will not be able to lie to this thing. You can't do it. But I beg you to try.

ROGER. Maybe you're overselling it a bit.

DR. DOLL. Oh yeah? You want to see our stats? How about one hundred percent? And the science is unassailable, there's almost no human-fallibility factor. I guess you could forget to turn it *on.*

Okay. Doctor: Have a seat.

(**WALTER** *moves, in a daze, to the hot seat, and* **DR. DOLL** *begins to carefully fit the headband onto him.*)

This is a Near-Infrared Spectroscopy. Have you worked with NIR?

WALTER. No. Roger, you knew / about this?

DR. DOLL. We're measuring neuronal activation. Specifi-cally, the increase in blood flow to your cerebral cortex which occurs whenever you *decide* to lie. Notice I said "*decide* to lie." You could be struck dumb on the spot, and I will still have captured the guilty *decision*. And it cannot be suppressed. By anyone. With the possible exception of individuals with delusional disorders, like…schizophrenia.

ROGER. Or Libertarianism.

DR. DOLL. You hear a lot about fMRI. There are guys out there now peddling fMRI as lie-detection. Oh, my God. Have you seen an MRI? How do you get a gen-uine liar into *that* thing? You'd be crazy not to plead claustrophobia. Talk about countermeasures. You want to know how to beat an MRI? Shake your head a little. But this thing, man, this thing, we shoot infrared light through your skull, you think a guilty thought, just *think* it, ventrolateral cortex activation, ding, we got you. Big red splotch on the monitor, big red image, says "Lie. There's a lie." We're gonna beat the god-damn terrorists with this thing.

ROGER. And Alzheimer's?

DR. DOLL. Yeah, that too. And soon we're not gonna need this headband. We can do this *remote – remote*, mind you, with an invisible laser and a hypersensi-tive photon collector, and you can put these at every airport checkpoint in the world. Courtrooms. Road-blocks. Wherever. People won't even know they're there. I mean, they'll *know*, but they *won't* know, right? Doctor, right now you're on the front line in the war on terror. Okay, we're about ready. Hold on.

(**WALTER** *is wearing the headband, a dozen wires merg-ing into a single strand, which is connected to the NIR unit.*)

(**DR. DOLL** *goes to the video camera, and turns it on.*)

WALTER. I don't want to be on the front lines in the war on terror.

DR. DOLL. You don't want to be on the front lines in the war on terror? Doctor, when you prove the perfection of this thing, and I'm – Well, if you're guilty, right? Goes without saying. But when you prove the perfection of this thing, the Pentagon is going to *bury* us in money. Not to mention private industry, right? Hold on.

(He returns to the video camera, stops it, rewinds, starts it again.)

Okay.

WALTER. I don't want to.

DR. DOLL. No, that's / understandable.

ROGER. Just relax, Walter.

WALTER. Roger, how / long have you…?

DR. DOLL. Shhh. Shh. Just a second.

(professional)

Okay. I am Dr. Doll. Roger Stanhope is also present, off-camera. The subject is Dr. Walter Kreutzer, employee of Chenoweth Security and Analysis. This is a real-world subject. Dr. Kreutzer has been accused of copying a secret internal memo and removing it from the workplace, and of, uh, of, uh, posting it, um, distributing it to, um, various media outlets.

WALTER. / I would like to stop the examination. I –

DR. DOLL. Secondarily, as a corollary to – Secondarily, Dr. Kreutzer will be questioned about his possible participation in a m– in an allegedly human-designed anthrax outbreak in the former nation of Rhodesia.

WALTER. Roger?

DR. DOLL. Additionally, there will be questions about alleged anti-Semitism and, um, unsavory associations – or, rather, associations that would be deemed / inappropriate for a CSA employee.

WALTER. This is not *proper*. This is / not a proper examin–

ROGER. Walter, it's fine. / This is not the way.

DR. DOLL. Obviously, the subject is distressed. I should re-emphasize that, unlike the polygraph, the spectroscopy is in no way affected by stress. So, the subject's obvious, um, anxiety should not be regarded as relevant. So.

(catching himself up)

Anti-Semitic, um – And *finally*, we will question the subject regarding his work with anthrax, and how it may be relevant to recent ruptures in security regarding the control of weaponized / biological substances. Okay.

WALTER. That's *outrageous*. It's *outrageous*. / I won't stand for it.

ROGER. Walter, it's a very brief examination. It'll be over in five minutes.

DR. DOLL. Now, Dr. Kreutzer…

WALTER. No! Roger, why are you doing this to me?

ROGER. I'm here to help you.

WALTER. You're not helping me! Nobody is helping me! / Everybody says they're helping, but they're not!

DR. DOLL. Doctor. *Doctor.* Let's focus, here. I'm going to begin the questioning now. I want you to answer each question with "Yes" or "No." Do you understand?

WALTER. Please.

DR. DOLL. It's okay. It'll be over in a minute.

The trial begins now. Question Number One: Is your name Walter Kreutzer?

WALTER. Yes.

DR. DOLL. Question Number Two: Did you copy a proprietary memo at your place of employment?

WALTER. Yes.

DR. DOLL. Damn it!

WALTER. I did it! Okay? I don't know why I did it but I did it!

DR. DOLL. Doctor, goddammit, you're ruining the / trial!

WALTER. It's what you want me to say, isn't it? / I brought it home because I could!

DR. DOLL. No. *No.* Wait for the questions. Please! / Will you wait for the questions?

WALTER. Because it was valuable and I wanted her to see it! To see it and tell me what to do!

DR. DOLL. I'm trying to…

WALTER. I hate her and I denounce her. But I fucking nodded. I nodded my head to say, "Send it!"

DR. DOLL. I need you to lie. Have I not made that obvious? Have I not made it clear to you what this is all about? I need you to *lie* for the machine!

WALTER. I looked her in the eye and I fucking nodded, like / a fucking idiot! I was disloyal, I'm a fool, I'm a traitor!

DR. DOLL. Stop! Stop talking! Sit still and answer the questions!

(**WALTER** *begins pulling the headband off.*)

WALTER. / But I won't do this. I won't – I won't –

DR. DOLL. Stop it! Stop that!

(He tries to restrain **WALTER.***)*

/ Stop it!

ROGER. Walter…

WALTER. I was disloyal! / I admit it! But I won't fucking *do* this!

DR. DOLL. Calm down. I'm going to call Security if you…

(**WALTER** *has removed the headband, and now tries to force it onto* **DR. DOLL***'s head, wrestling him to the floor.*)

Call Security! Call / Security! He's trying to kill me!

WALTER. Have you ever betrayed your own code of ethics?! Have you ever betrayed a friend?!

(**ROGER** *makes a call on his cell.*)

Have / you ever stolen anything from work?

DR. DOLL. Stop it! Let me go, / goddammit!

WALTER. Have you ever told a lie to protect / yourself?

DR. DOLL. Stop it! / Please.

ROGER. This is the sloppiest science I have ever seen.

WALTER. Do you dislike people / of other races?

DR. DOLL. Get off me!

> (**DR. DOLL** *escapes, tears the headband off.* **WALTER** *remains, spent, on the floor.*)

You son of a bitch. / You screwed it up. That's *it*.

ROGER. *(on phone)* It's time. Get 'em over here. I was going to say "hurry," but I think / we've calmed down.

DR. DOLL. *(mostly to* **ROGER***)* I *told* them, to have someone *here*! "What could happen?" "What could happen, in an isolated wing, with an insane person you just caught giving / secrets to his Islamic wife? Huh? *What*."

ROGER. *(on phone)* I don't think we'd better talk about that now. Let's wait on that.

> Yes, it is. It's weird. I'd say, "weird."

> Yep.

> *(hangs up)*

DR. DOLL. I told them this could happen. "We're stretched thin." "He's harmless." "We've got more important things to worry about than that *Dead* Man."

> *(to* **WALTER***)*

> *Dead Man*!

> *Now* look at me. I'm gonna be in a neck brace.

ROGER. Maybe you should get out, then.

DR. DOLL. *(to* **WALTER***)* You stay there. Stay right there and don't *move*!

WALTER. *(complacent)* Okay.

DR. DOLL. Asshole.

ROGER. So get the fuck out, then.

> (**DR. DOLL** *exits.*)

> Walter, you're bleeding.

(The knife wound has opened up, staining **WALTER**'s *shirt.)*

WALTER. Oh. Ouch.

ROGER. You know, just because he *said* the machine was perfect… You never know.

WALTER. I don't care. They got me.

ROGER. You could have turned her in at the start.

WALTER. I brought the memo home.

ROGER. They might have understood. It's an organization of self-interested parties. *Mercenaries*, for God's sake.

WALTER. I'm not a mercenary. I'm a scientist.

ROGER. That's where you got tripped up. That Rhodesia stuff. You got all mixed up, confused it with the real issue.

WALTER. What did we *do* there, Roger? In Rhodesia? What kind of people *are* we?

ROGER. Let me tell you something.

(He goes to the video camera, turns it off.)

Do you remember that night in Johannesburg, when you had that little get-together at your place to signal the end of a good run? But I had to work, so I showed up a bit late? Here's what happened to me on the way there: I'm driving up that road toward your house, and I'm on that long, empty part between the back of that supermarket and the back of that warehouse? You know where I mean?

WALTER. Yes.

ROGER. I'm driving along that stretch, and up ahead, this black woman is crossing the road. She's looking at me as I'm approaching, but she's not breaking her stride in the least. There's no intersection, no crosswalk, no stop sign, so of course I expect her to wait as I pass, but as I continue to bear down on her, I realize she has absolutely no intention of doing so. At the last second, I actually have to swerve to avoid hitting her. And as I go by, do you know what this woman does?

This sixtyish Bantu woman, in a kaftan? Do you know what she does? She gives me the *finger*. Not the devil's eye, not the horns, not the fist or the open palm or any of the other domestic and international gestures available to her, but the good old, American finger. America's export to the world, apparently. And I was outraged. I mean, I had the right of *way*. So, before I even knew what I was doing I slammed on the brakes, and I look in the rear-view, and she's just standing in the road back there, looking at me. No shame at all. So now I'm angry, and I think, "This'll get her attention," and I get my 9-mil out of the glove compartment, and I step out into the road with it, and I aim it at her. Just one hand, like a cowboy, you know? And you know what she does? She gives me the *finger*. So I fire the pistol. I'm fifteen yards away, you understand, and I'm firing with one hand, in the *dark*, no chance of hitting her, no chance at *all*, and I'm not even trying to, of course, but you know what? I got her right in the head. I think. I *think* in the head, I never actually found out. All I know is, she went straight down, *straight* down, like one of those demolished buildings, into a position too, um…*tortured* for a living person to endure. I was surprised by what I'd done, of course, and I looked around, and there was no one. I was alone. So I got back in my car, and I continued to the party, and I was quiet at first, you might recall, but very quickly I came to grips with a very simple fact: Nobody gives a shit. Nobody gives one shit.

Shouldn't that fill you with a sense of…freedom?

(DR. DOLL *enters.)*

DR. DOLL. Well, Dr. Kreutzer. They're here for you.

(blackout)

End of Play

A NOTE ON THE STABBING

I am conviced that Samira's stabbing of Walter in Scene 4 is only effective if the audience is surprised by it, an effect that would be spoiled by awkward staging or an unconvincing prop. Fortunately, I can pass along the ingenious solution devised for the Steppen-wolf production by director David Cromer and fight choreographer Joe Dempsey. I recommend it to anyone staging this play.

They started with two identical paring knives. They had the blade removed from one, and a magnet inserted into the handle. This magnetic knife-handle was hidden under the kitchen island.

Walter had a small metal plate sewn into his undershirt.

In the scene, Samira grabbed the real knife and stalked Walter around the kitchen, ending up behind the island. Just before the stabbing, she dropped her hand out of sight of the audience, tossed away the real knife, and took the fake one from its place. Then, she quickly "stabbed" the knife onto the plate on Walter's chest, where it held fast.

This effect was duplicated for the production at Asolo Rep, and never failed. Thanks, Joe and David.

— *J.W.*

OTHER TITLES AVAILABLE FROM SAMUEL FRENCH

MEN OF TORTUGA

Jason Wells

Drama / 5m

Four men conspire to defeat a despised opponent by a ruthless act of violence: they will fire a missile into a crowded conference room on the day of an important meeting. Maxwell, a hero of the old guard, volunteers to sacrifice himself for the plan. Then Maxwell meets Fletcher, an idealist with a "Compromise Proposal" designed to resolve all conflicts. Maxwell regards the Compromise as hopeless, but he develops a liking for Fletcher - a distressing fact when Maxwell learns that, if the conspiracy proceeds, young Fletcher will be among the dead.

As the scheme spins wildly into complication, the plotters descend into suspicion, bloodlust and raucous infighting, while Fletcher is drawn, inexorably, into the lion's den.

"Gripping…You'll be hearing more about *Men of Tortuga*, a blistering new play about corporate and government malfeasance from a Chicago actor named Jason Wells (who turned in the best piece of writing all year from a playwright.)…On one level, Jason Wells' elliptical drama *Men of Tortuga* is a genre-based thriller a la James Bond or Quentin Tarantino. But Wells is sufficiently skilled to dig deeper than that…taut sophistication…"
– *The Chicago Tribune*

"A highly original work…some of the sharpest humor you will see this season…both entertaining and thought-provoking…a must-see."
– *ChicagoCritic.com*

"The testosterone-rich quintet ripping apart the stage (literally) in Men of Tortuga makes the lads of Glengarry Glen Ross look like delicate hothouse flowers…brutally hilarious thriller…this twisted tale escalates to deliriously wonderful heights of violence and absurdity…Wells parcels out the story sparingly, keeping the audience on a need-to-know basis. It's a method that works perfectly in creating an environment that's at once profoundly ominous and patently ridiculous."
– *Examiner.com*

OTHER TITLES AVAILABLE FROM SAMUEL FRENCH

TERRE HAUTE

Edmund White

Drama / 2m

A famous author comes face-to-face with America's most notorious terrorist. One has a story to write, the other has a story to tell. As the clock ticks on death row, a strange bond grows between the two men. Filled with clever sparring and raw emotion, this is a taut drama that touches on the definitions of freedom and the need for love.

The *Daily Telegraph* in London hailed *Terre Haute* as, "topical, transgressive and thrillingly dramatic."

"White has captured the amusingly constricted voices of the patrician novelist and the plebian terrorist cannily and cogently."
– Charles Isherwood, *The New York Times*

"Provides us a concise and haunting retelling of the facts, plus an imaginative and realistic creation of 'what could have been'."
– *BroadwayWorld.com*

OTHER TITLES AVAILABLE FROM SAMUEL FRENCH

NELSON

Sam Marks

Drama / 3m / Interior

Nelson is the story of a young man caught between two worlds. By day, he works as a low-level assistant to a film talent agent. By night, Nelson is the camera man for an underground, gang-related videotape series. As the videos become increasingly dangerous and popular, Nelson develops an overwhelming obsession with a C-List actress. Eventually, Nelson's two worlds collide with disturbing, unsettling results. The play is a darkly comic look at the guilt dream of a man trying to find something authentic in a world of two very different kinds of film.

"Funny...Creepy"
– Neil Genzlinger, *The New York Times*

"Marks continues to offer a fresh urban voice. *Nelson* grabs your ear from the outset with its halting staccato street talk, and in the fine office scenes, Nelson's racist boss attacks him with a Mamet-like patter of disdaining sarcasm."
– *Time Out New York*

OTHER TITLES AVAILABLE FROM SAMUEL FRENCH

DUST

Billy Goda

Thriller / 4m, 1f, with doubling

Dust is an edge-of-your-seat thriller. Martin is an executive with money and a paunch. Zeke, a gifted young man torn down by drugs, is an ex-con with street smarts and a minimum wage position. Early one morning, in the fitness center of the Essex House, a battle-of-wills begins over the most trivial of requests. As described in *The New York Times* review: "Verbal sparring turns angry, posturing leads to entrenched positions, and out of nothing - out of dust - a grudge match is born." Once Martin's daughter Jenny becomes entangled, the stakes are raised even higher - escalating a war for respect into one for revenge and ultimately survival. Who will be standing when the dust settles?

"Great theatre! It's fun, it's exciting, it's electric, it makes you understand why theater is so special."
– WOR Radio

"THRILLS in DUST! EXCELLENT ACTING AND WRITING laced with mordant humor."
– *The Associated Press*

"*Dust* begins with a struggle over power and respect. Verbal sparring turns angry, posturing leads to entrenched positions, and out of nothing – out of dust – a grudge match is born. Billy Goda tells his story in short, sharp scenes, each with a clear dramatic idea."
– *The New York Times*

"Billy Goda's *Dust* revives the potboiler thriller!... Critic's pick"
– *Back Stage*

"NYC THEATRE PICK"
– *Newsday*

SAMUELFRENCH.COM